RESERVATIONS
No

No RESERVATIONS

AVA LINDSEY MORROW

No Reservations

Copyright © 2022 by Ava Lindsey Morrow. All rights reserved.

No part of this publication may be reproduced, stored in a retrieval system or transmitted in any way by any means, electronic, mechanical, photocopy, recording or otherwise without the prior permission of the author except as provided by USA copyright law.

The opinions expressed by the author are not necessarily those of URLink Print and Media.

1603 Capitol Ave., Suite 310 Cheyenne, Wyoming USA 82001
1-888-980-6523 | admin@urlinkpublishing.com

URLink Print and Media is committed to excellence in the publishing industry.

Book design copyright © 2022 by URLink Print and Media. All rights reserved.

Published in the United States of America

Library of Congress Control Number: 2022911111
ISBN 978-1-68486-214-6 (Paperback)
ISBN 978-1-68486-216-0 (Digital)

24.05.22

This work is for my precious children, Rebecca, Jonny, Sara, Mark. Luke, Jackie and my grandchildren Nate, Rosalie, and Carter.

1

The August sun came strong through the window. Mary smiled and slung her feet over the edge of the bed. "Gonna be one hot day in Georgia," she whispered to herself. Slipping on the clothes Mama had put out for her, shoes in hand, she tiptoed out the back door.

The day Mama had waited for had finally come. Getting together with family confused Mary. She didn't understand the stories that were told or why they were important. Sometimes conversations abruptly ended when she came close enough to hear. Mary didn't look like anyone in her family. She felt set apart even when her relatives greeted her with hugs. A sudden smile brightened her face. Sometimes they brought her gifts. She wondered how many would stay for her birthday. *I'll be twelve years old in a few weeks*, she thought. Mama always told her autumn of 1960 was a great time. *Is it because that's when I was born?* she wondered.

"Mary Victoria Smith, what in the world are you doing? Young lady, you'd better get yourself in here this minute. I have told you time and time again not to go outside in your church clothes. I get you all fixed and just look at you. Look at you! What am I going to …"

As mother chattered on, Mary tuned her out. Desperate for a moment to herself, she looked down. Mary had tried so hard to keep from getting her pretty clothes dirty, to keep from disappointing Mama. Looking down at the baby-blue dotted Swiss dress, she struggled to find a single spot of dirt. She stood frozen as Mama dabbed at her skirt, spitting on a tissue and furiously rubbing the thin fabric. Mama didn't notice the tiny particles of paper that clung to the delicate material. She didn't notice the last vestige of dignity that precariously teetered across her little girl's soul.

"All I want is a picture of my family. Just one little keepsake before you're all grown up. I try to get everything just right. You wait until your daddy gets home." Mama continued her fussing, lost in her own world of criticism.

Yes, yes, Mary thought, *when Daddy gets home he'll understand why I had to go outside.* The sun had come through the bedroom window that morning, pulling her out of bed, winking through clouds that floated in shades of red and pink. The birds lifted their heads from under their wings and sang like glory. The new day held a power that reached inside the dark room like a beckoning siren and drew Mary to her secret place. It was a private hideout, not much to it really, one board stuck between two trees. Still, the vines grew around the trees creating a lush green cave that hid her from the rest of the world. The tiny space had become a safe haven.

"Mary? Mary! Where is your mind, girl? Don't you know we've got to get going?" Mama jerked on the hem of the dress and turned Mary to face her. Grabbing slumping shoulders, she continued. "Will you ever listen to me?"

"I was thinking about that little squirrel, Mama. You remember, don't ya? I think I saw him this morning."

"Oh, Mary, please." Mama emitted an exasperated sigh as she continued to fiddle with the garment.

Layers of Mary's mind lifted until she could place herself back into the months of cold weather. She'd worked all winter trying to make friends with a scrawny little squirrel. He had looked poor and hungry, something that needed help. Sitting at the supper table, she would wait until no one was looking and hide bits of cornbread in a napkin. Later, after making up an excuse to slip outside, she'd offer the fare. At first, the shy creature ran when she threw the pieces out. One day, as the first snowflakes fell, his hunger got the better of him. She had him then. It didn't take long for the little fellow to trust her completely. After that day, he got to where he would take the bread right out of her hands. Mary had a confidant.

When Christmas rolled around, she took him a special treat of vanilla wafers. He liked them so much that he scurried down the tree trunk and sat beside her. The memory brought a slight smile across a sad face. "Mama," Mary asked, "don't you remember once I caught Daddy feeding him too?"

"Yes, and don't you remember what I told you about that little beast?" Mama stood to give her one more once over. Mary shrugged as if trying to brush away a spider web. She would not soon forget her mother's comment. Mama had said only a rabid animal would come up to people like that and insisted Mary stay away from him. She had no idea how much the child depended on him. It was one more thing that Mama didn't understand.

Trying to shake off her dark cloud, Mary struggled to continue a memory of good times. Wiggling and turning, she'd sit in her hideout for hours hoping no one would find her or disturb the solitude. Sweaters, coats, and mittens had protected from the cold, but her backside tried in vain to find comfort on the rough wooden plank. So often she wished to be a little squirrel that could run up and away into the treetops. Trouble was, she always knew she'd run farther than that if given half a chance. An overpowering feeling of a grander destiny consumed her as she sat on that board.

"I am Mary Victoria Smith, and I have no idea where I come from, or how I will grow up."

Once again Mama's voice interrupted. "Mary, Mary! I think you're ready now." Her voice softened. "Come on, dear. Daddy is locking up the house. Run and get your jacket. Please!"

A child's mind wished she could sneak away from her mother's fussing. Still, she found herself climbing into the car to begin their journey. She wished she was riding with Daddy in his truck. It smelled of his pipe tobacco, and, though the inside might look cold and hard, it was filled with his softness. Whenever she rode with him, he snuggled her close and didn't talk much. Daddy always saw the hawk flying over. Mary wondered if it was because he sat close to the window. Sometimes she imagined that the hawk had once been a special friend to him like her squirrel was to her. She liked to think of him as a little boy sneaking out bits of bread for the mighty bird and wished she had the courage to ask him if he heard the animals the way she did. It bothered her mother so much when she tried to ask her about things like that. Keeping silent was a survival technique that Mary had adapted to quickly. Unable to confide in her father, she sadly dropped her head. Though she felt a special closeness to him, she knew he too had learned silence. Someday, she vowed, she would find someone like herself.

It felt as though the car moved forever, though it traveled only eighteen miles of soft country road. Mary tried to sit still and think so she wouldn't bother her mother. Occasionally she looked out the window and wondered what was so important about the trip.

Her mother was preoccupied for a while. She concentrated on her driving and mentally clicked off her list of what she considered necessary for the day. Without warning, she turned to Mary and a frown crossed her face. "Just sitting there jiggling along like a little bowl of Jell-O," she said. "Don't you have anything going through your mind you could talk about?" She glanced back and forth between the road and Mary's stoic face.

Mary tried hard to come up with something to say. At a complete loss, she turned her gaze back out the window. She wondered if she would ever know what to do to make her mother happy.

"Well, I'll talk then. You know, camp meeting is a family tradition. Every August, on the first Monday after the second Sunday, family and neighbors meet at the campground for a week of prayer and praise. It's good for the soul."

The car tossed, forced over ruts in the dirt road. Mary mentally took inventory as the place rose in front of her. An open gate and a friendly sign, welcomed. Most families stayed in crude log structures. A few slept in tents. The Taylor house had two sets of huge bunk beds filled with down feathers. The table was big enough for the whole family to fit around. There was even a tiny front porch. Mary thought their house was the most luxurious until her bare feet hit the cedar shavings that covered the dirt floor. She quickly learned that the only thing worse than tight little black church shoes were splinters between your toes.

Mama was all smiles as she unpacked the belongings. After being reintroduced to most of the family, Mary was ushered out by some of her relatives. One of her aunts gave the young ones strict instructions to play until they were called back to the house. As Mary left, she heard her mama say, "This year I hope the Holy Spirit takes hold of both Mary and her daddy." Wondering what was meant by such a statement would have to wait for later. For now, Mary had child business to attend to.

Aunts, uncles, and cousins arrived, filling the house. Called too soon away from her playmates, Mary stood among the group looking into each face, hoping to find one similar to her own. She put on her best smile and faithfully bestowed it upon each person. Most of the faces wouldn't even smile back at her. She tried to believe it had to do with the feeling left over from last year. One of the cousins had already imitated the "fire and brimstone" sermon that had been the glory of the services. The poor little girl felt more lost.

The crowd stood, sweating and grumpy in the midday sun, for hours. A photographer arrived and attempted to pose the overlarge group. Everyone got tired. Tempers grew short. Some begged for a break. Without warning, the hymn "Holy, Holy, Holy" burst from inside one of the aunts. The crowd was startled and a bit embarrassed. Mama poked her sister in an attempt to chastise her. The portly matron would have none of it. She sang loud and a little off key, but she enjoyed herself immensely. The sound was infectious. Soon a few more worshippers were cautiously humming under their breath. Some of Mary's cousins giggled. Everyone looked to Mary's mom as if to ask permission to be happy. Her guarded smile allowed the assembly to quickly finish the torture.

After the pictures were taken, Mary was allowed to change clothes. "Hey, keep your church shoes on," her cousin Jim warned. Mary glanced at Mama standing with her people wrapped up in old stories and fond memories. Children anticipated their escape from the clutches of boring adults.

With his finger to his lips, Jim bade Mary to be quiet. "Wanna have some fun?"

Mary nodded.

"Well come on then."

A sense of freedom filled the child as she followed him down the hill to the big outdoor meeting place. It was called an arbor. Her eyes followed the tall poles that supported a roof pitched so high that the angels must have been the only ones who could dust the cobwebs off the corners. Every summer some of the menfolk would whitewash the poles, but the boards making up the ceiling were left in their natural state. The dirt floor, covered with hay, made for great sliding.

The children ran way up to the top of the hill. Faster and faster each would seem to fly until they hit the arbor edges. Once the slick soles of Sunday shoes hit the hay, each one went down in a pile of crashing bodies. Some of the bigger kids could slide up to the front podium. Watching from the sidelines, daring to get her courage for another turn, Mary noticed a new group. "What' up?" A skinny, pimple faced boy asked.

Jim smiled. "A little action in the old town today."

"Action?" The boy and his entourage smirked. "Sliding in the hay is fun for you?"

Jim nodded, pointing to the children still playing.

"You're messing up the floor. There is a service starting soon."

"So," Jim said. "We'll fix it."

Mary turned to notice the hay had been pushed together in places leaving spots of bare dirt. Small particles of dust drifted in the sun beams like fairy magic.

"There's hay stuffed under the piano. The preacher is gonna have a fit."

Mary moved to Jim grabbing at his elbow. Someone began to sneeze. A fat little boy let out a rebel yell. Legs pumping and arms flailing he ran between the benches. For a moment his form was fabulous. The next yell he uttered was one of fright as his feet hit dirt. Flipping and fighting for balance the youngster landed against the piano. The extra hay didn't save him.

"Well. Would you look at that. His head split open like a ripe cantaloupe."

Jim raised his fist. "You sorry son …"

"No," Mary cried. "He's bleeding."

"What?"

"That little boy is bleeding. His head is bleeding." Neither noticed the group of boys slink away.

Jim raced toward the injured child. "Hey buddy. You okay?"

The child grinned "Did you see? I was the best. Did you see me?"

"I saw you. It was good until you hurt yourself."

"I ain't hurt. I knocked the scab off my head. That's why I'm bleeding. My brother hit me a couple of weeks ago. Mama thought I needed stitches, but I'm too tough for that."

Mary gasped as the little boy stood up and brushed off his pants. "Your brother hit you?

"Yeah," he said, pointing at the retreating bullies.'

"Boys play rough, Mary." Jim grinned at her.

"A little too rough for me." Thinking it best to get away from the action, Mary wandered away looking form safer amusement. Around the back corner of the arbor, she noticed an odd face in the camp meeting scene. It was an older man, who she'd seen earlier picking up trash around the grounds, leaning against an enormous oak. He was dark skinned, but not like the other people she was used to, and his jet-black hair reached down past his shoulders. Colorful beads adorned his neck. She was more than curious, but the calls of other children prevented her from speaking to him.

Twilight turned to darkness far too soon for Mary. Her restlessness led her to peek through the boards in the tent house. The sound of her father's voice made her squint harder through the cracks. Startled, she caught a glimpse of her daddy speaking to the dark-haired man that so intrigued her. They stood quietly smoking their pipes. Desperate to know what they were saying, she pressed her ear tightly against the wall, but their words floated away in the smoke that softly escaped up to the clouds.

2

The next day service after service filled the hours. Most of the children came to dread the sound of the conch shell blown to signal the starting. Mary was glad to realize the evening meal would put a stop to the preaching for a while. When the minister came to eat with the family, Mama tingled with excitement. For the womenfolk, it was some sort of honor to have him there. For Mary, it was one more chore to endure. Grandma's fried apple pies weren't tasty when they grew cold during a ten-minute blessing. Spying through her prayers, Mary realized she hadn't seen her daddy at the gathering. *He slipped away*, she thought. Into her plate, she grumbled to herself, "If he doesn't have to be here, then neither do I." The grown-ups, about to give another a turn at prayer, gave her the perfect opportunity. She waited for each head to bow, each reverent eye to close, and then quietly exited the room.

The smell of pipe tobacco guided her. It took a moment to discover the men squatting outside the glow of the porch light. Looking around for a way to eavesdrop, she decided to climb the brittle mimosa tree while straining to hear the men's words. It struck her as odd that her daddy would sneak away from the family. He dutifully attended church with Mama when they were home. He'd agreed to take time off work to spend a week with them. Yet, she noticed he kept distant from everyone Mama appeared to love. Something very strange was going on. She felt she had to be a part of their meeting, so she pretended to fall from her catlike perch. The unceremonious landing that would have sent Mama into hysterics was not acknowledged with as much as a lift of either man's brow. It dawned on her then that they had been well aware of not only her presence but also how long she had been there. *Will they include me in their conversation?* she wondered. It didn't matter really; it was enough to be in their presence.

Daddy casually looked over and said, "Ernest, this is my daughter, Mary." He gestured toward Ernest, smiling, deeply proud of his child.

Mary looked hard at the man. He was not as old as she had first thought, though his face seemed to come from ages past. His eyes looked so deep inside her that she felt he instantly recognized some part of her that no one else had ever bothered to understand. Mary found herself staring back at him, sensing that his look could bring fear to many. A strange sadness for him brought tears to her eyes. He stood tall, a man who knew his purpose. When he spoke, his voice had a low, melodic sound that was at once soothing and haunting.

Later, lying in bed, Mary wondered about the man. It would be the first of many times that people would appear to know her and embrace her being. Thoughts were becoming muddled with tiredness and half-dreams. Almost ready to sink into slumber, Mary heard her mother shouting.

"You mean you let that drunk Indian get close to my Mary! Have you lost your mind? Did he touch her? Did he say anything to her? He didn't tell her one of his crazy stories or—what does he call them—visions of the spirit world?" All of a sudden Mary was jerked awake by her mother's hands tightly gripping both of her shoulders. "They can't have you! You are mine now! They can't have you, do you hear?" Then she began to sob.

The next morning, at least to Mary's eyes, Mama seemed to have forgotten the events of the night before. What Mary would never know was the extreme act of strength of will it took for Mama to pull herself out of bed that day. She had promised long ago to try to push away the feelings of inadequacy that had been placed upon her by the constraints of Southern society. Mama went into town with her sister to restock supplies. Piled into a beat-up Buick, they laughed like school girls as they left. No one who heard the shouting the previous night brought it up.

The women had been gone ten minutes or so when Mary caught sight of Ernest near the arbor. Moving down the hill to get a closer look, she noticed that he had a single blade of grass in his hand and was looking intently at the hard-packed ground. With racoonish curiosity, she meandered toward him.

As she got closer, she saw that he had placed his piece of grass into a tiny hole in the ground. The hole was about as big around as a pencil. Silently creeping closer so as not to disturb his concentration, she was surprised as he suddenly jerked something out of the hole. Her brow wrinkled as she watched him put something in his front shirt pocket. His appearing to speak to whatever it was was the final straw. She had to ask.

"Whatcha doing?"

Ernest looked up and grinned, "Fishing for grammer hammers."

Mary wiggled her nose and asked, "What's a grammer hammer?"

Ernest leaned over, pulling out his pocket so she could see what was inside. "Look yonder, girl. Can you see it?"

"Yuck. That's the ugliest excuse for a worm I ever saw. What ya gonna do with it?"

Standing tall again, Ernest wore a hurt look on his face. It was lost on Mary as she stared down at the ground for more worms. Finally the child glanced up at him. "Gonna catch me some dinner," he said.

She stood with her hands on her hips, thinking. "Oh, I get it. You gonna use it for bait. That ugly worm?" She shook her head negatively. "Well, I can get you better bait than that. I know a spot to go digging. You can get the biggest, juiciest worms you ever saw. Handfuls of 'em."

"Only need to catch one fish. Only need one worm." With that, he abruptly turned and walked toward the creek.

Mary looked around at the holes, amazed that she'd never noticed them before. They were everywhere. The ground was completely smooth, and she wondered how deep the worm house went. "If he can do it, then I can do it." She searched for the blade of grass that Ernest had been using. No matter how hard she tried, she couldn't manage the capture. Lost in frustrated concentration, she didn't notice Daddy walking toward her.

"Fishing for grammer-hammers, are you?" he questioned.

"Yeah. Can't seem to do it though."

"I guess I'd better show you how. First you gotta get the right kind of grass, and of course you gotta hold your lip right … " The two spent the afternoon "fishing" and finding tiny living creatures in the grass. It was a time of sweet communion. Her gentle daddy opened a new world for her. Pointing deep into the grass, he spoke softly. "Look, Mary."

"What is it?"

"A lady bug." Daddy bent down and let the tiny bug crawl across his palm.

"Can I hold her too?"

"Sure, but be careful. Don't squeeze her. Just let her run over your arm."

Mary giggled. "It tickles," she said. "Oh, Daddy, she flew away."

"I reckon she's got a family to get back to. Did you thank her?"

"Thank her? For what, Daddy?"

"She gave us a fine afternoon of play, didn't she?"

Mary nodded, a smile lighting her face. They had been so intense that they hadn't heard the conch shell blow and only noticed the service starting when the women filed down toward the arbor. "Guess we better go find a seat?" Mary spoke as if she had a ticket to a lynching.

Ruffling Mary's hair, Daddy winked. "Look for your friends," he said. Arm in arm they followed the faithful and found a seat with the family.

After that, Mary was never bored in the outside church again. Close by Mama, she appeared well behaved while searching from hay to ceiling for tiny creatures scurrying about busy with their lives. It struck her that maybe these loud men preachers were looking for God in the wrong places. Even so, many years later, she would have to admit that she had found the Father during those camp meeting days. Something told her that Ernest would understand her sentiment.

3

The rest of summer stretched long and lazy. Time was spent helping Mama do various chores. One of Mary's favorite jobs was washing the pollen off the outside chairs. The water ran yellow, and it made Mama happy to have everything clean and in order. When the washing was finished, Mary was occasionally allowed to play with the garden hose. July in Georgia was a time when any kind of coolness was welcome. Sticky with sweat, she hosed herself off and watched the pollen roll down her little brown legs and pool in the driveway.

With Daddy at work, Mary tried hard to focus on her mother. She made an effort to understand grown-up thoughts and feelings. She'd noticed a distance between her parents. Imagination took over, and she decided her mama needed a friend. Mary found herself trying to teach her mother to play. With a mischievous grin, she turned the garden hose, blasting her mother's toes.

"Mary Victoria, what in the world are you doing?" Mama slipped off her sandals and wiggled her toes in the muddy grass. "Thought you needed a little cooling off." Mary giggled hopefully.

"My, my, if you don't sound just like your daddy." Mama stood staring at Mary. A strange expression crossed her face.

Mary was uncomfortable. She felt like she needed to pass some sort of inspection. What did Mama expect to find with her probing eyes?

Mary began to roll up the garden hose. Her stomach made a loud roar.

"It's getting hot now." Mama said. "Do you think we could make a little picnic to eat out back?"

"That would be fun."

Mama tapped Mary's cheek with her finger. "I happen to know there is some fruit in the house. It's already been washed. I think a little cheese and a few crackers might stop your grumbling." Mary blushed.

"Thing is," Mama continued, "my feet are all wet and my shoes are soggy."

"I'll get it," Mary offered.

"Bring a big towel and a pitcher of water too."

"Okay." Mary smiled not realizing the easy camaraderie Mama fought to create was fragile.

When she returned, Mama smiled. "Morning chores are done.

Think you can rest a little while after your tummy gets full?"

"I'm not a baby, Mama."

"I know. You've grown like a weed, Mary. Still, a little afternoon peace is good for you. After we clean up, go to your room. Take at least thirty minutes to be quiet and still."

Knowing it was useless to argue, Mary nodded. When her time was up she cracked the door to her bedroom and peered out.

She heard Mama's humming coming from the kitchen. "Mama?"

"In here, Mary. Her voice carried an invitation.

Mary walked into the kitchen.

Yards of pale-green fabric lay on the kitchen table. Excitement exuded from Mama's voice as she spoke. "Mary, I've had an idea. Look at all this material. There's enough for two dresses. Can you believe it?"

"Two dresses?"

Mama pulled a box from the closet and started digging through the contents. "Yes, one for you and one for me." She held out a thick envelope. "It's a pattern, Mary." Mary stared.

"It's a dress pattern. I haven't looked in these boxes for years. You've grown enough that I'm sure these old patterns of mine will work for you. I'm going to make us both a dress."

"Two dresses." Mary feigned a cough to hide her grimace.

"Oh, Mary, don't act that way. Look at this. The bodice will fit close and the skirt will be full. Remember when you were a little girl and would spin around in your church dress? You thought yourself so pretty."

"Are you making a church dress?"

Mama giggled. "I guess I am. A grown up version of a pretty little church dress. We'll look stunning."

It was evident that Mary's mother very much wanted the two to look alike. It was a difficult task since Mary's skin tanned dark in the summer sun while Mama's stayed lily white. Mary's body was thick, her back broad. Mama was small-boned and appeared fragile. Still, the more they looked alike, the more Mama felt secure.

Soft brown curls adorned Mama's head, and one of her favorite activities was going to the beauty parlor for a perm. One day she decided to introduce Mary to the world of smelly chemicals and trivial gossip that filled the shop. It was a day that Mary would never forget. Black hair, almost down to her waist, was pulled into a plaited pony tail. Mary had never considered cutting it. She wished it would grow down to her ankles. Mama, however, had a different idea.

The thick braid held high, Mama said, "Mary, you need to cut off this mop of hair." She looked at the beautician as she continued, "Betty, don't you think it'll grow faster if she keeps it trimmed?" She and the beautician shared a conspiratorial wink.

"Climb up in this chair, honey. Let me see what I can do for you." Betty beamed at Mama. Mary didn't believe them about having her hair cut, but she and Mama were becoming friends. She did so want to please. Slowly she climbed into the chair. The hairdresser pumped the seat higher and higher in an attempt to reach her subject better. Mary sent Mama a look of pleading. She didn't like anyone to touch her hair. Her mother should have known that.

Mama stood behind Mary and gently lifted up her braid. She said, "Right about there should be fine." The view from the mirror allowed Mary to see Betty the shearer nodding her head like a drunk puppet. The lady snipped off the braid, leaving only a short stubby edge against the collar of Mary's shirt.

Horrified, she jumped out of the chair. Something inside her wouldn't let her cry. Mary had begun to notice Mama often whispered things to Daddy. When that happened, he smiled a sad smile, retreated to his chair, and pulled a newspaper in front of his face. He never showed anger, never offered hurt for hurt. His calm diminished Mama's tirade. If Daddy could manage control, Mary decided she could too. She took a deep breath and forced her eyes to open as wide as possible lest a tear be squeezed out. Finally, silently, she sat back down. So betrayed, yet she had to sit there listening to the clip, clip, clip of the scissors as Betty evened up the ends. The noise was torture.

The next words out of Mama's mouth were, "I think I can spare enough of my grocery money to let you have a perm, Mary." She dug in her purse and pulled out a worn billfold. Smiling, she nodded, while Betty dug for little pink curlers and black shiny combs.

When the deed was done, Mary stared at herself in the handheld mirror that Betty provided. Two sets of fingers fluffed and combed her hair. "I just don't understand it," both women muttered. Mama continued, "I've heard about a perm not taking, but I guess I didn't believe it." Her head bobbed back and forth in amazement.

Mary couldn't help but feel a slight happiness that though her mother had cut her braid, no power on earth could make it curl. As if to console herself, Mama spent the afternoon repeating over and over how much more comfortable Mary would be with a short cut. Each parroted reminder stung deep inside Mary's heart. Her hair was such a part of her being. She longed to understand why her mother couldn't know that.

Daddy came home to a house pulsating with tension. His only acknowledgement was to hug his two girls.

"Have you seen my newspaper? It wasn't in the yard," he said.

"It's by your chair, Daddy. I brought it in for you."

"Thank you, Mary. Did you and your mama have a good afternoon?"

"I, we …"

"Look at her. Isn't she pretty?" Mama beamed.

"As beautiful as she always is," Daddy said popping open his paper.

It brought some peace to Mary for him to ignore them.

"You're not related to Samson, Mary. Losing your hair shouldn't be that great of a problem." Mama's voice was over loud.

Mary turned as Daddy lowered his paper and shook his head sternly at Mama. Her voice abruptly stopped and with it her teasing. Relief washed over Mary's heart.

The next morning the sun, totally unmindful of the pain a little girl suffered, shone brightly and clearly. The previous night Mama had carefully put an outfit on the bed for Mary to wear. Big plans were under way for the day. Mary longed for an escape. There would be no lounging and stretching in bed. Sharpened shards of light forced her out of her dreams.

"Mary, oh Mary, are you up, dear?" The bedroom door was pushed open. A smiling face appeared. Mary winced at the thought of matching hairdos. "Get up. Get up. We've got to go." Mama pulled the covers so hard that she jerked them right off the bed. "Oh, great, now I'll have to remake the bed. Try to hurry?"

Even the prospect of an additional chore couldn't dampen Mama's spirits that morning. "I've got a surprise for you!" she yelled as she walked through the hall.

Putting on her clothes was about as easy as enjoying a last meal. Mary tried to force herself to be happy and to hurry. She tied her shoes and leaned across the bed to grab a wayward pillow. Covers pulled up, long fingers gently smoothed all the wrinkles away, and Mary hoped her mother would be satisfied. She then trudged toward the kitchen for breakfast.

On the table was a small white pocketbook that exactly matched the one Mama carried. It was "the surprise." Mary fingered the smooth leather and opened it to see if anything was inside. "Do a few chores around here, and maybe next time there'll be a little money in there," Mama offered as spoonfuls of eggs and several strips of bacon were plopped on a plate. "Try to get your breakfast down so we can get along."

"Yes, ma'am." Mary chewed a bit. "Are we walking?"

Mama considered. "I want to, but hurry. It's so hot already."

Mary shoved her half-eaten food away and stood. "If we're walking, I'm ready."

"You are so like your father," Mama said. Again she looked oddly at her child. Mary wondered what it was she was trying to see.

The tree-lined street was a pleasure. Perfume of honeysuckle mixed with the smell of the onions that had been growing in the fresh-cut grass. Slowly ascending the last hill, Mary and her mother took a break at the stop sign.

"Whew"—Mama wiped her brow—"it sure is hot. Hope it's worth the trip," she said mostly to herself.

"What we shopping for, Mama?"

Continuing on, Mama's delicate hands floated through the air, insinuating nothing or everything. "I'm shopping for a new belt. We both need one for the dresses I'm sewing. Of course," she said with a wink, "I really just want to look." "Look at what?" Mary persisted.

"I don't know exactly, Mary. Browse. Haven't you ever heard of browsing? It's something women like. Shopping is relaxing."

"Seems to me it'd be better to make a list, come get what you want, and go home." Mary's footsteps dragged as the fear of a dreadful day filled her.

"Mary, I just thought we could have a little fun today. You don't ever seem to be happy. Next time I'll come by myself." Mama marched into the clothing store with the air of an army commander. Mary stifled a smile. The thought of being left home was most appealing to her.

Wandering through store after store, rack after rack was exhausting. "Can we go yet?" Mary asked.

Mama turned around, her face red. "Do you have any idea how many times you've asked me that today?"

"You're not even looking at belts."

The purse in her mama's hand began to jerk. She shoved it up to her elbow almost breaking the strap.

"Mary, go outside and wait for me. Walk up and down the sidewalk, whatever. Just go." Mama stopped short of shoving the child.

Once outside, Mary grazed the sidewalk. She'd already been through the dime store and drug store, and having no need for the grocery store, she thought about crossing the street. She looked at the signs. Those storefronts weren't inviting either. Only three other people appeared to be out that morning. Mary decided to walk the few blocks to the barber shop. She'd been there a couple of times with Daddy and knew there were chairs outside. At least she could sit if she went up there.

Staring down at her toes, Mary almost bumped into a lady. Upon looking up, she was astounded by her appearance. The woman had on a long, brown skirt and a bright red blouse. Her silver hair was tied up in a bun. Several necklaces of beaded jewelry made her look like the gypsy in a picture Mary had seen in one of her school books. The beads caught Mary's eye. Something about them was familiar.

Without saying a word, the woman drew the child to her.

"Your tears will make you strong," she whispered. Ever so slowly, she walked away. In the brief moment that Mary looked down, she disappeared completely.

"How strange," Mary spoke to herself. Her fingers strayed into her short locks. She hadn't cried, at least not where anyone would know.

Beginning to push away what she held in her heart was the only way Mary knew to survive. Camp meeting had increased the knowledge of Mama's God. Daddy and Ernest delighted in a world of animals and flowers, even bugs. Daddy took his family to church, sat stiff and stern during the service, but allowed a giant picture of Jesus to hang above his and Mama's bed. "Still," Mary whispered to herself. "He doesn't close his eyes when we pray. Do they have the same God?" Lost in her confused musings, Mary wandered down the sidewalk. "Why didn't you tell me you were going to walk so far?" Mama stood overburdened with packages. "Why are you standing there staring out into space? We can go home now."

"Mama, I was talking to a lady." Looking up the sidewalk for the old woman was useless. Anyone dressed so outlandishly was sure to draw attention in the backward town. Where could she have gone? There were no corners to turn, no doorways to disappear into. "Where did she go?"

"I don't see anybody. Please come on. And help me carry something. Half these things are for you anyway."

"But, Mama, didn't you see her? She knew things about me. She told me I was about to blossom. What do you think she meant, Mama?"

An odd look crossed her mother's face as though she had been struck by a forgotten idea. She touched Mary tenderly and smiled in a way that frightened the girl. "Let's go home, sweetheart. I need to fix supper."

Dutifully, Mary followed in her mama's footsteps. The image of the woman she'd seen haunted her. Her skin had been dark, not like some of the maids in town, but like Mary's. The woman approached Mary as if she knew her, cared for her. Mama claimed she didn't see her, but how could that be possible. Mary's mind raged. *Mama had been desperate to make them look alike. Why?* An idea entered her mind.

4

"Mary, get up." Her bedroom door opened a tiny crack. Smoke rings billowed across the thresh hold."

Daddy, what are you doing?"

"Lazy days are over, princess. Today is a school day."

Mary smiled, stretched, and got up. "I know. I can't wait to see everybody again."

"I made extra coffee in case you need it."

"You're silly, Daddy. You know that stuff is awful."

"Not to me." Mary heard him laugh. "You decent," he asked, pushing the door more open. "I brought your little purse. Mama said…"

She stood in front of the mirror running her fingers through her short hair. Her face was bland as she reached for a hair brush. "Um, here's your purse. Mama said you had new clothes to wear."

"I do," Mary answered. She smiled at her reflection."

"That's nice I suppose. Hope you have a good day."

"I will. Don't worry, Daddy."

He dropped the purse on the dresser and kissed the top of her head.

"I put some lunch money in there for you."

"Thanks, Daddy."

He hesitated. "I've got to go to work, princess. You tell me all about your day when I get home."

"I will." She brushed through her hair as her daddy left the room. "You too," she said as an afterthought. Mary rushed to the kitchen, picked up a piece of toast, and waved at Mama. Going out the door she heard the whoosh of bus brakes. "Bye," she called, mouth half full. If her mother answered she didn't notice. Mary was bursting to tell someone her news. The only one who could remotely be called her friend was a little girl named Sara. "Sara," Mary said. "Guess what. I've got something crazy to tell you. " Both girls were about to explode by the time lunch break came. Sara's curiosity couldn't stand any more, and she practically pushed Mary through the lunch line and over to a chair.

Sara pleaded. "What's your secret?"

Leaning across the table, Mary announced, "I don't think Mama is my mama." She sat back like a satisfied cat.

The saddest look crossed Sara's face. She struggled to hold back tears. "But that means you're adopted? I can't believe you told me that. I'm so sorry, Mary. How could you stand to know your real mother didn't want you?"

Mary stared at her, unable to understand why Sara would say such a thing. Her real mother didn't want her? She had not even entertained such a thought. This was a crippling blow. *My mother didn't want me.* Mary walked home from the bus stop. Her head drooped so low that it felt like her chin was glued to her chest. For once, Mama noticed her despair.

"Mary, what's the matter? Did something happen at school?"

"No, Mama. I just feel bad.

Her hand on her child's forehead, she said, "You don't feel hot. What made you feel bad?" She pulled Mary's chin up to face her. "You know you can tell your mama."

Intense feeling rushed through Mary. Here was the chance she had longed for. She prayed her mother would understand. Gulping, she tried to hold back a sob. Tears, silent and caustic slid down her face. The eyes of a child looked deep into the heart of a woman.

The two made their way into the house. Mama sat down in her chair and pulled Mary onto her lap. Long kisses were planted on the top of Mary's head Mama held her tight. "Your mama loves you. You know that don't you? No matter what happens in the world, you mama loves you."

Mary shook her head. She felt too mixed up inside. There was no way she could bring herself to confide her secret thoughts. She recognized the fact that her mother, in her own way, was trying to ease her pain. It was the kind of love Mama had that was hard to understand. Mary needed to learn to take it out of her head and run it through her heart before she could find its worth.

"Do you have any homework?"

Mary shrugged.

Mama caressed her hair. "Maybe you should go to your room for a little while before supper. You seem tired, Mary"

Mary shrugged again and stood up. "I'm going outside for a while. I need ..."

"A moment for yourself?" Mama offered.

"I'm going outside." Mary's mind felt numb. She didn't know what was happening in the world. Mama called her a dreamer, but she had no idea what that meant. She walked without direction and was surprised to end up at her secret place. She couldn't remember the last time she'd ventured there.

The sun was warm on her back. She tried to relax, to pull the heat all the way to her soul. She tried to pray, but like her daddy, her eyes refused to close. Her mind was filled with confusion. She gazed into the trees. A slight breeze teased the branches until they danced apart creating an open canvas of sky. Shadows moved. Mary rubbed her eyes and inched her body forward to see. To see, what? She mused. A picture of herself shimmered into view. She was in a house that wasn't known to her, and she had a tiny white rabbit in her arms. She knew this rabbit wanted to be outside. He wasn't wild, and she feared for his safety. She put him in the window, right up next to the screen, hoping that seeing the outdoors would be enough. It made him even sadder to see his dream and not to reach it. She loved him and wanted him happy, but she couldn't let him go to his death. There were all sorts of animals out there waiting for a juicy morsel. Even if he got past them, how would he find the food and water that he needed? No, it would be much better for her to keep him safe. The poor little fellow almost mourned himself to death. She had shown him the world but kept him apart from it. Was it concern or selfishness that held him prisoner?

One day she came to the window, and he was gone. The screen held no sign of his leaving, and she was sure someone had let him go on purpose.

The vision filled her with anger at the unknown person who was so intent on ruining her pleasure with her little white friend. The memory crept into her dreams. Sleeping became difficult as she tried to make sense of what she'd seen. The anger began to eat at during the day. She seemed to have somebody trying to teach her a lesson that she didn't want to learn. The meaning of the message filled hours of her time. Finally she saw there were two sides to herself: one selfish and petty and one loving and concerned for others. She had to choose which one to be. *Where had the thought come from? Some stupid wish for rabbit couldn't produce such a fantasy.*

Sometimes after such an experience she would wake up calling her father. He would sit with her, rub her back, and tell soothing stories.

One night, after the distressful vision, her daddy got called to come help pick up someone who had been hit by a car. The call scared Mary; she didn't know why he needed to go. When she saw Daddy early the next morning, he bore a great weight of sadness. "Daddy, what happened last night?"

"Ernest was hit by a car last night."

"Ernest? The man I met at camp meeting?"

Her father nodded.

All over town that day people talked of the drunken Indian killed up at the big curve. Folks said he had been staggering through the night chasing some sort of critter. Daddy took Mary aside after supper. "I want you to know Ernest never touched any kind of drink. I've known him for a long time. He was a man in tune with a world that most of us don't comprehend, so we make fun of it and try to hide our fear." Daddy smoothed out Mary's hair, appreciating her unusual lack of interruptions. "Baby girl, I think Ernest had a good heart. He liked you. I'm sure he'd want you to know he was now in a better place to help watch over you." Daddy pulled her close to him. His thoughts carried him a million miles away.

Mary didn't understand and didn't know how to get Daddy to explain it to her. Later she heard people around town say that when Indians die they only want to be around their own kind. It made her wonder why Ernest had so desperately called out for her father.

Most of the next morning was gone before Daddy came home. When he came back through the door, he hummed a tune that sounded like "Amazing Grace," but every once in a while he would sing words that Mary had never heard before, words that came from another language, another time, words at once sad and comforting. About to invade his solitude, Mary noticed Mama in the room with him. She paced from the window to the bed. Her voice was soft, but Mary knew something was wrong with her. Finally she sat beside beside Daddy on the bed cautiously reaching out for his hand. Mary couldn't hear the words they spoke, but she felt her daddy wanted forgiveness for something. He put his head on Mama's shoulder, and they held each other tight.

For an instant, she thought she should be part of their circle, but then something told her she was at her perfect place for the moment as the spectator.

Always hating the silence of others, wanting to know everything at once, now Mary saw her parents differently. The silence embraced her like a warm, smooth coat. It gave her a part of herself that she had sought for so long.

5

Mary began to think more and more about whom she might be related to and, for the first time, looked forward with special interest to an upcoming family reunion. Mama was happy too, though she sure complained about all the work involved. Trying to stay out of Mama's way was impossible. Over and over she bellowed for Mary's help. From the looks of what had to be packed, Mama must have been planning to have to feed an army.

"Mary, do you see that box over there?

"Yes, Mama."

"Bring it over here. We've got to get this food loaded so Daddy can get it in the truck." Mama made a loud sigh of exasperation and turned herself back to her list.

Moment by moment, the mountain of food grew in size. Creamed corn, green beans, tomatoes, squash, okra, and cantaloupes from Daddy's garden overflowed in a never-ending stream.

"Mama, is this all?" Mary asked, struggling to put dishes into boxes.

"No, Mary, I'm gonna stir up some biscuits when we get there. That way, they'll be nice and hot."

Daddy walked in. He and Mary exchanged smiles. Wrapping his arms around Mama's waist, he pulled her close. "Did I hear something about your biscuits, I hope?"

"Yes, and turn me loose. I've got too much to do to fool with you."

"I like that," Daddy said as he feigned heartache. "I was thrilled to hear about your biscuits. Nobody in this county can come close to your fluffy puffs of dough."

"Yeah, Mama, everybody knows that," Mary added.

"Well, I thank you for that, but if you expect a taste, you'd better get that truck loaded so we can be on our way." Mama wrung out her dishrag and smiled to herself.

"Hey, Mary," Daddy said as he tapped her shoulder and pointed to a pan almost hidden from view. "Know what's in there?" Mary snuck over and tried to peek under the foil.

"Careful, don't open it. Just let your nose figure it out."

Mary took a deep whiff. " Chocolate cake?"

"I think so," he teased. "Come on. Let's pack it up."

Long after Daddy and Mary thought they were finished loading, Mama kept looking at her list and checking off items. The truck was packed so tightly that they wondered what could possibly be left for anybody else to contribute to the affair.

No Reservations

When the family got to Grandmother's sprawling old house, the bigger kids were called to help set up the card tables and chairs outside. The smaller children were instructed to place table cloths and silverware on each table. Unable to count how many people were there, Mary stood impressed at the mass of tables. Some were overloaded with food; others held sweating pitchers of iced tea so sweet you could use it for pancake syrup. A few tables were placed in the shade of oak trees for folks who had to sit a while after their meal to let the food digest. Cool mountain air took the punch out of the late summer sun. A pleasant feeling crept over the gathering. Children darted back and forth everywhere while adults talked about how Lucy's boy had grown and whatever happened to Aunt Jenny.

When everything was in perfect order, the dinner bell sounded loud and clear with sound that signaled the time to come together, beginning with prayer. Everyone held hands in a circle, bowed, and gave thanks to God for keeping each one safe and healthy and bringing them together again for another year. It was a time of connecting, not only with each other but also with the past. The warmth of love filled every hand.

After dinner, Mama spent part of the afternoon with her cousins and sisters trying to identify pictures. They had a big box filled with old photos, cards, and letters. Some of the cards were much prettier than any Mary had seen in the town drugstore. The box smelled old, and the women took great care to make sure nothing was torn or lost.

Mary's Aunt Margaret pulled out several pictures and handed them to Mama. "Look at these. Are they the same person?"

"Yes." Mama seemed to ponder as she looked closely at the photograph. "That's Papa, don't you think?" Mama questioned as she passed the picture back to her sister.

"Wonder what year this is? How old could he have been?" Margaret sat back in her chair deep in thought.

Some lady that Mary didn't recognize pulled up a chair and looked over Margaret's shoulder. Her eyes squinted nearly closed and her nose wrinkled with concentration, she announced with authority, "That's Marvin all right. I'd recognize that nose anywhere. Don't know what year it is though. He looks right young, don't ya think?" She snatched the picture from Margaret's hand. Peering closely at it, she continued, "That's Russell with 'em. That Russell had the finest head of red hair I've ever seen. Shame the picture's a black and white." She continued to stare at the likeness as if trying to conjure up the long-lost day that it had been taken.

The women passed a few of the pictures around. Mary struggled to find a face that in some way could resemble her own. "Look at this lady," she said. "She's dressed up. What did she do?"

"She was a teacher, "Aunt Margaret answered. "Lots of our family were teachers. There were some who felt they had helped shape the future."

Mama and her family smiled at each other. The pride among them was good and well deserved. Mary felt honored to be a part of it.

Later, the women recalled the strength of times past. They talked about their men who had gone to war. Mary listened closely to her aunts' conversations. She noticed that there was as much pain in remembering the ones who came home as the ones who didn't. To say good-bye to a brother, father, son, or husband must be a horrible thing. Included in the box were many pictures of men who appeared to be standing stiff and stoic in some sort of uniform. "They look so handsome and so brave," she commented.

Grandmama sat down heavily in a folding chair. "You may think they look brave, Mary, but they were really just frightened little boys that were forced to do a horrible thing." She thumbed through some of the photos. "Many of them," she continued, her eyes far away and misting over, "longed for the laps of their mothers." Her words created a gentle quiet that settled over the group.

Digging deeper in the memory box produced gasps of delight. Mama found an old diary written when she was about Mary's age. "Mary, come sit by me. You're always wanting a diary. Bet you didn't know I had one." She carefully separated the pages. "Listen here. The date is December 28, 1942." With a deep breath, her eyes fighting tears, she began to read. "I got a chocolate bar for Christmas. I tucked it into a little box. I'm going to eat one bite a week and see if I can make it last all the way to Easter." Mama closed the book and shut her eyes as she spoke. "I would let small bites melt on my tongue," she said almost to herself. "I wanted to savor each morsel."

Mary was touched as she watched her mother reminisce. Slowly she began to realize what was meant by the terms *making do* and *getting on* with next to nothing. It began to dawn on her how much these hardworking people appreciated what they had.

Then, as always happens to women who talk about loss, the tears began to fall for their children. A few had children taken by fevers or accidents; others lost before they took a breath. Some of the women, like Mama, mourned for babies who could never be.

It was this rush of emotion that caused the women to separate and seek out their families. Many kisses were placed lovingly on precious brows. Mama patted Mary's cheek and slipped her hand around her child's waist. Her loving touch encouraged Mary to walk with her to find Daddy. It would soon be time to begin the chore of packing up and going home. For another year, all had heard the stories, shared the laughter, and cried the tears. Each left better for the doing. It made them feel a part of something bigger than themselves. It was called family, and Mary gloried in it.

After the reunion that year, Mama began to go to her mother's almost every Sunday for dinner. Mary grew close to her Grandmama but wasn't privileged to visit her Grandpa much. He was always in his bed with a vinegar poultice on his head. He wouldn't even talk to Mama. After a while, everyone learned to leave him alone.

6

Grandmama's house had originally been built upon rock pillars, and it was still possible to crawl all the way under her porch and come out the other side. It was always cool beneath the porch, but the adults warned the young ones not to go too far under lest the whole thing come down on them. At least a dozen cats made their home way back under the house where no one could reach them. One day Mama told Mary she could have a kitten if, of course, she could catch one. It was one of those statements that a mother wishes she had never made.

"Grandmama?" Mary asked as she sprawled across the great dining room table. "You ever touch one of those cats?" Mary knew her grandmama fed them scraps almost every morning.

"No, honey, they're too wild to play with. Your grandpa used to like 'em out in the barn 'cause some of 'em were good mousers." Grandmama chuckled as she spoke. "They used to follow Grandpa when he was milking since he was fond of squirting a little milk their way." She shook her head as she continued, "That was many months ago before he took to his bed." She sadly turned her attention back to her biscuit dough.

Mary couldn't help thinking how much she wanted a kitten. Figuring, like her squirrel, that they would probably come out for food, Mary devised a plan. She saved up her chore money and bought the smelliest, fishiest food available.

The next Sunday, armed with the food she'd bought, she initiated the plan. At first, she sat way up on the hill with absolutely no results. Casually, she plucked tiny daisies and wound them into a chain. Frustration set in as Sunday after Sunday passed and she couldn't even get the big cats to come out of hiding and sniff around the food. Finally, one rainy afternoon, a few of the old toms trusted enough to try a little of the concoction. Almost ready to give up, Mary noticed a mother cat coming timidly toward her. The feline kept a watchful eye, but Mary never moved from her perch. Soon the coy animal ignored Mary's presence. Over the next two months, the food pan was gradually moved farther from the house. It was a great day when all the grown cats were eating close enough to touch.

Weekly offerings were continued as Mary waited patiently for the time when the mama cat would feel secure to bring her kittens with her. Sure enough, as the stifling heat of summer turned into the coolness of fall, fat little fur balls appeared. Smiles of delight slid across Mary's face when she realized the kittens had been too small to come out any earlier.

Bounding into the house after petting the mama cat, Mary couldn't contain her excitement. "Grandmama! Grandmama, I touched the mama. I touched the mama!" Breathless she nearly shook her grandmother's arm off.

"Touched her? I am amazed." Grandmama wiped her weathered hands on her apron and smiled. "Guess you saw the babies too, didn't ya? You know they're born with their eyes tightly shut and have to nurse constantly for several weeks."

"I know, Grandmama, but they came out too, right behind their mama. And you know what, three of 'em don't have tails. Isn't that funny?" Mary had to struggle to control her excitement.

"Lordy me. I saw a tailless cat around here a while back. I thought somebody did some meanness to him. You think he was born that-a-way?"

"Yes, I saw it in a book, Grandmama. It's a special breed. Manx."

Grandmama stood amazed. "How do you know that, girl? Are you gonna try to catch one of those kind?"

Mary sat at the table and picked at a bowl of sweet plums. "I don't know, maybe. Have to take whichever one I can get."

"Be patient. I know you'll get one. Go on with you now. I've got work to do."

"Don't want me to help you?" Mary questioned, all the while hoping that her grandmama wouldn't take her up on the offer.

A deep smile split the wrinkled face. "You're a sweet, darling girl, but I'd rather you play. There'll be plenty of work for you in your life. I guarantee that."

Mary smiled too. "Can I take a handful of plums with me?"

"Yes." Grandmama turned to her work. "Good luck to you," she slung over her shoulder as Mary dashed out the door.

Mary climbed back up the slight hill above the house and watched the kittens play. She looked them over, deciding her favorite was a tiny little yellow-haired one. He was not only cute but also full of fire. She wondered if it would be possible for her to ever get him. His mama was protective of her babies. "Hey, Mama Cat. You're a good mother, aren't you? Can I have a kitten? I'll take care of him forever." Mary crept away and patiently bided her time.

Week after week the family traveled to the home place, as Mama called it. Gradually more family joined them. On some occasions Mary had playmates for the first time in her life. She enjoyed the companionship.

One Sunday afternoon she was disappointed to find her cousins had stayed away due to chicken pox. All the women went into town together, Daddy dozed on the front porch, and Grandpa moaned in his bed. Patience had worn thin and left to her own devices, Mary decided today was the day she would capture her kitten. The smell of approaching rain meant her cat hunting time was limited. When they came out to eat, she decided to make her catch, knowing she would only have one chance. Readying herself by taking a deep breath, she slowly moved her arm into the perfect position. Then, with a quick lunge, she had him! The little devil tried to claw her arm off! The other cats scattered, their earlier distrust fully restored.

Mary held the little kitten as close to her body as he would let her. For a while, as she rubbed the top of his head, he struggled. He relaxed ever so slowly. With her index finger, Mary stroked him under his neck. As the first raindrops fell, she sneaked into the house with the little bundle and curled up on a bed with him tucked under her chin. He felt safe. The rain came down in soft melody as her little kitty purred. Mary smiled, happy with her victory. Now she had a friend to tell her dreams to, who could come into the house, who her mother wouldn't accuse of being rabid.

The next morning Mary listened to Mama and Daddy talking. They were outside the house. Mama's voice sounded sharp and irritated. "What in this world are you doing?" she asked.

"I's cutting a little hole here."

"Why?"

"So Cat can come and go. That way he can get outside when he needs to and we won't need a litter box. Good idea, don't ya think?"

"I can't believe you would actually go to the trouble to make a special door for a cat." Mama looked up as Mary stepped outside. She spent over an hour shaking her head and telling Daddy how silly he was. "Mary, I think your daddy has lost his mind." As she went back into the kitchen, Daddy looked up and winked.

For a while, Mary felt guilty for taking the little kitten away from his family. Sunday after Sunday she watched the felines sicken and die due to their wild living. She found some peace and slowly became more comfortable with her decision to steal him from them. Daddy always made her feel good about bringing Cat to a better home. In time, even Mama began to baby Cat a little when she thought no one was looking and would give him a hug.

After finally getting a cat, Mary's attention turned to other things. Her grandfather stayed in his room. He seemed alone and sad but not very sick. Secretly she thought that, if he would get rid of the smelly vinegar poultice, he would probably be up and about in no time.

One cool quiet Sunday afternoon, while everyone else took after-dinner naps, Mary pulled a straight-back chair into the room and sat next to Grandpa's bed where he lay sleeping, to wait him out, just like she'd done her cat. He pretended not to look at her and emitted rude grunts from time to time. Then he rolled over and turned his back to her. Mary sat waiting for almost two hours for any other response. She watched his even breathing and noticed the rag on his head had dried. He had on a copper bracelet, and his skin under it was a greenish color. He wore a white long-john shirt, and she wondered what kind of pants his blankets covered. The hair on the top of his head had thinned almost to the point of nonexistence. A faint whisper of brown that wasn't wiped out by the whiteness that age had brought him still lingered about his temples.

After a time, Mary thought she heard her mother calling. "She's looking for me," she casually said to her grandpa. A battle waged within her over whether she should answer Mama or not. There was no way to tell what her response would be to Mary being there. Quietly, Mary stood and walked toward the bedroom door.

When Mama caught sight of Mary, she smiled. Mary was astonished. She could never guess what emotions would run through her mother. It seemed even stranger when Mama grabbed her hand and pulled her back into the bedroom.

"Papa, would you turn over and look at my child?"

At first, Mary thought he hadn't heard. His movements were almost imperceptible. The grunts and moans that usually resounded throughout his house were silent. Then she noticed the covers around his feet were twitching. All of a sudden his legs moved with such force that in an instant he was sitting up staring at the two. He was a big man, and for the first time, Mary noticed how he dwarfed the bed in which he lay. The bones of her mother's face mirrored his with precise perfection. They shared the same long nose; if he could still smile, the picture would be complete. Mary suddenly knew that he would never smile again. Mama was beauty and light; he was darkness and destruction.

An evil tone rose out of his mouth as he straightened himself and spoke. "The girl is not your child. She is not a part of us. Not of our line." He stared straight into Mama's face, searching for signs of pain his words produced within her heart. Mary looked at her too, hoping to see some sign that would tell her what to do.

Mama held herself erect and proud. She tilted her head ever so slightly in his direction. She was in command here, and they all knew it. Softly and precisely, she spoke. "You are right, Papa. She is not of your line. She will never suffer your abuse or meanness. I will forever shield and protect her from your curse. She is my child, not coming from under my heart but from inside it.

That she will carry nothing of you is a great comfort to me."

Still holding Mary's hand, she left the room with the grace of a queen. Mary later wished she'd had the nerve to look back at the old man. She would forever wonder about the effect of her mother's words.

Stopping briefly in the hall, while still holding Mary's hand, Mama bent down close to her ear. "Don't ever go in his room again. He's not worth your curiosity," she said.

Mary tightly held herself in control. Still she thought a lot about Grandpa in the following week. What would make him dislike her so? Mama's words had been strange. What could they mean? She had to know.

7

Several dark rain-filled weeks passed before the family returned to the grandparents' house. Mary had begun to wonder if they would ever go back. She missed her grandmother and wanted to question her. When they finally made another visit, Mary found Grandmama outside in her garden. She took great pleasure in her little treasures of color. She still carried her treasures from her walk back to the house after her early morning wanderings in the orchard. Her pockets were full of pecans, and she and Mary moved in easy friendship.

"Go on up to the picnic table, Mary. We'll crack these nuts up by that anvil."

Mary watched her grandmother's strong wrinkled hands cracking and helped her pluck the meat from the nut. They sat munching and enjoying the cool, soft breezes.

"Grandmama, why doesn't Grandpa like me?" Mary asked.

"Oh, Mary, I don't think you need to think about your grandpa. He's just sick and tired is all," Grandmama said.

"Well, he doesn't like Mama or Daddy either," Mary continued.

"Honey, your grandpa never really wanted your mama to marry your daddy. In fact, they almost got into a fight on the day of the wedding." Shaking her head sadly, she continued, "I don't think you need to know all this. It has taken me many years to convince your grandpa to let you visit. Let's take pleasure in that, okay?"

Muddled thoughts rattled inside Mary's head. She had come to love her grandmother and enjoyed the aunts, uncles, and cousins who sometimes joined the family gatherings. Yet, she desperately needed to know why her dear, gentle daddy would fight his new bride's father on their wedding day. The questions kept coming to mind, making her determined to get answers.

Mary began to ask questions of her relatives, though always careful to watch their postures and retreat at the first sign of discomfort. Some of the best information came from Aunt Margaret as she was standing at Grandmother's kitchen sink cutting corn one morning.

"Aunt Margaret, why doesn't Grandpa get up?" she asked, continuing her work. "Aunt Margaret, do you like my daddy?" She stood still for a moment. "Aunt Margaret, why is everybody so sad when we come? What happened when my mama and daddy got married? Aunt Margaret, do you like me?"

Margaret's patience wore thin, and she decided the best way to get rid of Mary was to answer some of the child's questions.

"Sweet Mary, of course I like you. I love you, for heaven's sake. I know you're such an inquisitive child, but some of it is too painful to speak. Aren't you a little young to be worried about people getting married?" She put down her knife and looked hard at the girl. Mary stared back at her.

The silence grew long and uncomfortable. It pushed Margaret into speaking. "You know I guess I always wanted to believe in love at first sight," she said. "I suppose every woman does. That's what it was like for your parents. When I saw your mama and daddy meet for the first time, I hated the way he looked at her. It was as if they were long-lost lovers, joyous in the reuniting. It made me sick to discover that no man would ever look at me in that way. I knew I was too plain. I had to be satisfied with watching them and wishing I could have that kind of love." Margaret pulled a chair out from the table and sat down. Tears sprang to her eyes as she continued. "The beauty was ruined by our papa. He hated your daddy, and I never understood why. Your daddy had just been discharged from the service. He had a good job, a nice disposition. Papa couldn't let your mama go, I guess. Maybe it was because she was the first. You know they say there's a lot of pain that a first child suffers that the younger ones never have to know."

"Oh, come on, Aunt Margaret. We both know it was because of his Indian blood."

"Mary, that's ridiculous! Indian blood, my eyeteeth! What kind of silly story are you trying to make up?" She chuckled as she dried her hands and left the room.

The rest of the story of her parents' meeting came to Mary from many sources. She didn't know what to make of it. Was it a tragedy or some sort of ironic comedy? Mary sat quietly in her room stroking Cat one afternoon while she put the bits and pieces together in her mind. Over and over she repeated the story to herself.

Mama arrived at the church that day wearing a pale-pink dress. It had a full skirt and a belt cinched at the waist. She was so small that Daddy could have fit both hands about her middle with room to spare. Her thick, shoulder-length hair had a redness to the brownness of it. She had her little white Bible clutched in her hands to give her strength. She and her friends were trekking to Mountain Town to give testimony to the people there. Mama and her group planned on going to the square-dance hall to speak.

Mountain Town had a rough reputation. The young people expected to find drink, bad language, and all sorts of heathen rituals, but they had faith that their God would keep them strong. Mama was full of youthful self-righteous determination. She had a sense that after this trip her life would never be the same as it was before. She felt fear mixed with excitement. The hope of making a change in the world was the motivating force. Daddy's brothers had talked him into coming to the party. He still sported his short air force haircut and his time in the service had turned a wiry, skinny youth into a strong, self-assured man. He had seen more of the world than he ever wished for, and some of life's lessons left scars upon his heart, but the truth of himself never faltered. Everyone thought he had become too serious and needed a little goof-off time. *Heck, why not?* he had thought.

The square-dance hall was in a giant warehouse. Boxes stacked in the back of the building provided a platform where the band set up. The caller needed to be above the dancers to direct the scene. The music was loud and the air thick with cigarette smoke, hot bodies, and whiskey breath. It was odd to notice whole families in attendance. The sound of laughter could sometimes be heard when the band took a break. One would almost imagine harmless fun was the theme of the event.

As the night wore on, only the serious dancers could maintain the pace. The families departed, leaving those young people who had found their partner for the night and those who became a part of the music. Each moved in their love dance. Soon the tunes became less familiar. The beat of a drum set the pace, and the words of the songs were coming from the ancients. At the height of the fury, Mama and her Bible-thumpers walked in. It was as if the sun had fallen from the sky. All eyes turned to the misfits. The curious gave way to the ludicrous. As the music slowly began again, Mama and her band of angels were pulled into the sensation. They could no more convert these people than they could stop their own conversion.

The music flowed around Mama, making her dizzy. Slowly it invaded her mind and into her soul. The drumbeat somehow felt as if it were coming from deep inside her. Her heart picked up each beat.

Daddy, thinking he had some superior knowledge of the world, moved in to help the ladies. His polite movements were ignored by these young girls who, for the first time in their lives, had let go of the regulations set upon them and were awakening to the feelings the drum produced. Daddy was intent on getting these pretty children, dressed up in adult clothes, out of his world and back into their own. These worlds mixed only with volatile results. He did well until Mama's face came into his view. Then, ignoring the command from his brain, his arms went around her. Their bodies moved with the drumbeat and each knew they had found the complement of the other. Though Mama finally got back into the big Buick to return to the church, they both knew they belonged together forever.

The next day Daddy came down from his mountains in search of the pretty little girl; when he found her, her world flipped upside down. Funny how in the end he gave up much more of himself than she did. She lived in a physical world of seemingly endless hard work and dreary days. Her papa had children for the purpose of supporting himself. The more children he had, the wealthier he could possibly become.

No Reservations

When only three weeks later Mama announced that she planned to be wed, her papa lost his senses. She was the oldest and should set the example for the others. Back then you didn't run off to some whore-infested dance hall and come back saying you would marry in a month. He beat her savagely in an attempt to control her. It only made her strong.

Rain clouds broke at the hour of Mama's wedding. Each fat droplet must have fallen from the sad eyes of an angel. Mama wore a pale-blue gown that lightly brushed her toes. With the marks of her father's hand still upon her face, she walked gracefully down the aisle to her love. Her head held high and her hands unsteady, she wished her parents could bless the union.

Her mother had defied her father and sat in the back of the church in hopes of making a fast getaway when the ceremony concluded. As the groom kissed the bride, the back door of the church opened and a sad, tired man that was once her gallant papa uttered his curse: "God above will punish you and may you never raise your children upon this earth." With all eyes upon him, the shrunken old man retreated. The door closed lightly instead of the slam everybody expected. It was the soft sigh one hears at the close of a book that has touched the heart.

8

After learning the story of Mama and Daddy's meeting, Mary thought often about her parents' lives. She was ever watchful for some moment, a grand display of dignity like the one she'd witnessed with her mama and grandpapa. She found herself disappointed. For all appearances, Mama was a simple woman who did the same things everyone else's mother did.

Mary thought back to the day Mama had taught her to make a bed. She'd been so frustrated by the insistence to do it right. Everything always had to be in perfect order.

"Now, Mary, I know you can do better than that. Smooth out the covers and tuck in the edges so that the corners make a crisp fold. I have told you time and time again, if something is worth doing, it's worth doing right."

Boy, don't I wish I had a nickel for every time I heard that in my life, Mary told herself. She had been made to make the bed three times that morning until it was picture-perfect. After Mama left the room, she had the evil urge to take a flying leap upon the mattress and yank those crisp corners into an infinite crumpled heap.

Instead, forcing herself to be pleasant, she'd followed Mama to the kitchen and asked, "Is there something else you need me to do today?"

"Well, Mary, do you think you could dust the living room? I mean really dust. Pick up everything off the tables, dust very well, and arrange the knickknacks so they look cute. I don't want to come back and see that you skimmed around the edges. Remember if it's worth doing..."

"Yeah, yeah, Mama, there goes another nickel into the cookie jar," Mary said under her breath.

She was startled as Mama turned as she left the room and said, "What, dear? Did you say something?"

"No, Mama. I'm just talking to myself."

And so the morning went until Mary could stand it no more. Everything Mama required seemed so picky. Why did it matter if her trinkets were arranged neatly on the shelf? Why did she insist on the bed being made? It would only have to be turned down again in a few hours. And why was dust such an abomination to her world?

Mary marveled that her mother actually appeared happy while she did these meaningless tasks, especially when she was in the kitchen. She would spend hours cooking something that would take ten minutes to devour. The endless monotony of work seemed to absolutely thrill the woman.

Finally, her list of chores done, Mary was allowed to escape to her own devices. Her mother's voice rang in her head: "Don't eat anything that will ruin your dinner." Mary promptly ran out to the strawberry patch. It was her sweet taste of revenge.

When she rounded the back corner of the house, she saw Daddy working on his tiller. He tinkered with it, turning it off and on and checking something about the motor. For a long while, she watched him, waiting for the right moment to talk to him. A thousand questions rattled around in her mind. Still, she needed some answers and was afraid to talk to Mama anymore. Mary believed her daddy would be truthful, but she also knew he was unable to tell her anything that could bring her pain.

She followed him down to the garden as he struggled with his machine, trying not to ruin the grass as he walked. They picked the beans and dug up potatoes. Daddy teased her about eating all the strawberries and tickled her in an attempt to keep her away from the muscadines. It turned into a playful and satisfying day. Long ago Mary had discovered that Daddy was happiest with a little dirt on his hands.

Ready for a break, she pleaded, "Daddy, can we sit for a while?"

"In a minute. I'm about finished. Go ahead and talk if you need to. You look like you have something to say." He yanked a few struggling blades of grass out of the tomato row and turned an eye toward the squash hills. Mary wondered if he were paying her any attention and, in desperation, cleared her throat a couple of times to get his attention.

"Daddy, do you know anything about my real parents?"

Daddy stopped his work and looked sadly at her. A gloved hand dragged across his brow and threw a rivulet of sweat into the garden. "I know everything there is to know, Mary. We are your real parents. We have done all it takes to be real parents."

He wouldn't look at Mary, and she got the impression that he was lying. Quietly pondering, she decided to question in another direction. She stood there for a few minutes digging in the dirt with the toe of her shoe to get her courage up. With great nerve, she asked, "Daddy, are you an Indian?"

This time he stared straight at her when he spoke. "Mary, most folks don't know what to say about that. My grandmother was what people call a full-blood. She was Cherokee." He paused, shaking his head as if in apology, and then continued. "I know a lot about Cherokee ways, but some days I don't feel very connected to my people. I made choices in my life that make it difficult."

"Is that why you went to help Ernest?"

"Sort of, I suppose. I had to be there."

Mary moved close to hug him. "I heard you singing. I thought I knew the words, but they were different from anything I've heard. What was the song you sang?" She nudged him and asked, "Daddy? Did you hear me?"

"Yes, Mary, I heard." He looked up into the heavens, not sure how to answer. "It was a song my grammy sang to me years ago. It came back to me at Ernest's funeral. It was the right time, I suppose."

"Will you teach it to me?"

"Maybe ... "—his pause seemed infinite—"... when the time comes."

"What if the time never comes?"

"You are such an impatient little girl," he said as he rumpled her hair.

"Daddy, am I an Indian."

"You are what you are, princess."

"That really doesn't help very much."

He chuckled before speaking. "Did your mama tell you how special you are?"

Mary nodded. "All the time."

"Never forget it!" The two worked around each other in the garden for a while then plopped down in the grass to gaze at the sky. Daddy loved the game of picturing things in the clouds. He could imagine other worlds up there and tell grand stories about them. Mary could listen to his words for hours. Slowly the times of his family would sometimes seep out, and she would wish she had the courage to ask him why she'd never met them. As their bodies reacted to the warmth of the sun, both relaxed. The melody of his tone changed, and it dawned on Mary that he was remembering instead of imagining.

"Ah, Mary, it's times like this when I think about being a boy. You know those big, fluffy homemade biscuits your mama makes?" He didn't wait for an answer but continued staring at the clouds. "My mama

No Reservations

made the worst biscuits you ever tasted. And she always made pans and pans full. I wondered what happened to them after breakfast." He was suddenly quiet.

Mary couldn't stand it. "Did you ever find out?" she asked.

"Find out what?"

"Daddy!" Mary tried to playfully slug his shoulder. "What your mama did with the biscuits?"

"Yeah." He grinned. "Want me to tell ya?"

"No, never mind. I'll just lay right here until I die of curiosity."

She stopped short of sticking her tongue out at him. He began his story again, laughing at what Mary wasn't sure. "One day I had worked all morning, and I was sitting on the creek bank gazing upward, like we are now." He paused again. "I hadn't meant to take such a long break, but my bones turned lazy, and I lay still and enjoyed it. After a while, I heard such a ruckus I knew I was bound to be in trouble. I heard my papa screaming and saw him stomping through the pasture. It seems an old cow had gone off and hid to have her calf. Papa was worried about her and had searched long enough for the worry to turn to anger. He was yelling and cussing that old cow, saying she and her young'un could go ahead and die out there in the lonesome for all he cared. Then suddenly he came hightailing it toward the water. He had come around to being stupid and kicked an old tree stump." Daddy sat up and scratched his head. Mary almost feared he had decided not to continue the tale. Looking down at her, he grinned even broader. "Everyone knows that's where bees make their nest."

She nodded encouragingly.

"I thought it a good idea, when I saw what was after him, to follow his lead." At this point, Daddy couldn't talk for laughing. Mary could well imagine him and his papa jumping in that shallow creek and praying those bees would fly right over. As their senses settled, she reminded him that the story started about his mama's biscuits.

"Oh, yeah"—he chuckled—"I forgot, and that's the best part! Papa was furious when he found Mama out on the other side of the pasture. She had her apron pocket full of those horrible biscuits, and that old cow would follow her into Hades for them. For all of Papa's yelling and flailing of arms, all Mama had to do was nod her head and the whole herd, led by old Betsy, would trot along beside her. I don't think Papa ever quite forgave Mama for those bee welts on his shoulders."

Daddy laughed, happy with his memories. Mary was glad they had become her memories too. After that, he began to speak more and more of times in his life. There were many events in his growing-up years that he hoped he could prevent his child from ever having to experience. He had suffered from brutal hard work, been cheated, abused, put down, and dismissed. Still, he had a strength that few men possessed and some people killed over. It was what made him a forgiving, loving man. He strove always to be the best he could be.

No Reservations

He often threw that challenge out to Mary, a little girl struggling to find her way.

Supper that night was later than usual. Daddy and Mary had stayed outside almost until dark. Mama, for unknown reasons, decided to put a candle on the table. The half-light of the room brought with it a feeling of comfort. They all enjoyed the mood. Deciding to take advantage of the calmness, Mary mentioned her curiosity about Daddy's family.

"Daddy, Mama, I love going to Grandma's house. Don't I have another grandma? I mean, Daddy told me about his brothers once. Where are they?" Looks that she didn't understand crossed her parents' faces. Daddy seemed almost pleading. Mama sat there looking stern and, for the first time, resembled her father.

Mother's eyes bored into Daddy's as if accusing him of planting ideas. He dug into his soup beans.

As Mary was about to speak again, Mama interrupted, "Mary, Daddy's family isn't the sort that you need to associate with."

"Mama, how could that make sense? You love him, don't you?" She stared at Mama, trying to figure out what she'd meant.

"Yes, Mary, I do, but Daddy and I decided a long time ago that it would be best to leave his people behind."

Mary watched Daddy take measured forkfuls of his meal, never lifting his head, pretending he wasn't the focus of the conversation. She couldn't stand it. "Daddy, what's wrong with them?"

His head jerked up with a vengeance, but his eyes softened as he looked at his bride. "There is nothing wrong with them, Mary. They live life a little differently from what your mama is used to."

"They always have a gun strapped to their hips," said Mama. "They're dangerous. I won't have my child around such people!"

"But, Mama, you've been overjoyed to get back to visiting your family. Why can't Daddy visit his?"

"I told you, Mary! They are dangerous," Mama exploded. She snatched up her plate and stomped out of the dining room. Mary and Daddy heard a crash that sounded as if she'd thrown it roughly in the kitchen sink.

Mary and her daddy finished their meal in uncomfortable silence as Mama came back and forth from the kitchen to the dining room snatching up dishes of food. Daddy winked at Mary, making her wonder if he hoped to figure out a way to win Mama over. At bedtime, Mary, with curiosity taking control, struggled to sleep. The whole situation puzzled her. Still, she drifted off, hoping for the best.

9

In the next few days, Daddy did talk Mama into visiting his family. Mary never knew what he said to her, but when school was out in June, they drove north for over four hours. For Mary, the trip passed quickly because she slept most of the way. As they neared Daddy's home place, the worn-out shocks on the truck bounced her awake on the dirt road. The forest was so thick that it felt as if they were passing into a cool, dark cave. Massive limbs grew out of giant trees, creating a pleasing canopy overhead. Mary stretched and looked around. She smiled. She liked the place already.

When Daddy took a sudden left turn, Mary was surprised to discover how much of the land ahead had been cleared. Acres of fields stretched out before her eyes. In the distance, she could barely make out what appeared to be a tractor. Daddy slowed his truck to a crawl. As they inched across the land, his smile broadened, and Mama's body stiffened.

Suddenly Daddy slapped his leg with excitement and exclaimed, "Look! Look yonder! I think that's my baby brother, Cal!" Daddy eagerly leaned over the steering wheel, squinting into the sun. As they approached the young man, his blank expression turned joyful. Mary noticed tears coming into both men's eyes. Cal ran to meet the truck and practically jerked Daddy from his seat.

"Hold on there a minute," Daddy said. "Gotta put this thing in gear."

"Finally come home, did you? Mama's gonna have a fit when she sees you."

Daddy hopped out of the truck and walked away with his brother. Mary and Mama wondered if he had forgotten them. Mama reached across Mary's lap and blew the horn. Her face was clouded with anger. Daddy merely turned for a moment and motioned for them to follow him. Grudgingly, Mama pushed down the brake and kicked open her door. She offered her hand to Mary. They stomped across the field after Daddy and his brother. Mary had a strange sense of foreboding.

As it happened, Mama had been more than right about Daddy's people. That very afternoon Mary realized with a shock how important guns were to them. Daddy, on more than one occasion, had taken her to the woods and pointed out little footprints. Sometimes he would hide among the leaves until Mary found him. It was obvious that he had spent a lot of time outside as a boy, but until that day Mary hadn't known he'd spent it as a hunter. He never told her he had been an expert marksman.

The bawdy family was a new experience. They loudly extolled all of Daddy's adventures. Mary watched him swell with pride. For a while that afternoon, he and his brothers spent their time shooting clay pigeons. Daddy never missed even when they started letting two go at a time. He placed his rifle against his shoulder with such precision that everyone stood and watched, mesmerized by the action.

Cal slapped Daddy's shoulders and led him toward the house. "It's getting dark. Thought some of us could go out tonight."

Mary watched her father prop his gun against a tree and cross his arms. She moved closer to hear.

Cal continued. "It's deer season."

"I am aware," Daddy said. "You know I can't go with you. It was hard enough coming for a visit."

"We'll be back before anyone knows we left." Cal spit hard into the ground. "It's what we do. Haven't you missed it? I saw you shoot today. You came here for something, didn't you?"

"I came for my daughter." Daddy straightened his back and walked away. "I need to tend to her and her mother."

After Daddy tucked Mary into bed, she lay there awake for hours anticipating the hunt the next day. Sure she wanted to go along, the wee hours of the morning found her still tossing and turning in excitement. She strained to hear any noise that signaled it was time to go. Finally, movement could be heard in the back of the house. Mary tiptoed toward the sound and saw her father move quietly down the back steps. She wanted to be brave and walk out with him, but something told her she wouldn't be welcome. She secretly followed the men as they moved away from her grandmother's house.

Tracking them through the woods, she couldn't help but feel that Daddy would be proud that all his lessons, done in fun, resulted in such an expert. Suddenly the men disappeared into the shadows. Anticipation caused tiny beads of sweat to begin to form on the palms on her hands. She was ready, but for what?

As the sun rose in the red and purple sky, Mary became acutely aware of the sounds about her. Just as some humans awake slowly, so seemed the forest. There was a comforting feel in the place. For a moment, time could suspend itself like the peace we feel in our prayers. Mary settled against the bottom of a tree, wondering how many mornings the old, mangled limbs had witnessed. She couldn't wait to see the deer family. Her mind's eye imagined the soft caress of the doe as she mothered her fawn.

Mary's back straightened when she heard an explosion. The noise of the guns was deafening. Men were yelling, and the sounds of them crashing through the underbrush destroyed the solitude of the morning. More shots, screams, and a chase was on. *What in the world is happening?* Mary wondered. She found herself running toward the clatter. And then, she saw the doe. She lay on her side, breathing heavily the last breath of life. A single shot, probably fired in mercy, had ripped through the top of her head. Mary didn't see a fawn and hoped with all her might that there was none. It would be too cruel to leave the poor creature without its mother.

Hiding behind a tree, she watched the men begin the work of field dressing in preparation for taking the deer home. Mary found the whole display brutal. The gentle creature was being pulled apart, and Daddy was helping. She ran stumbling, crying, back toward her mama, the prim and proper lady who would disapprove of such sport. *How can they destroy such a beautiful creature?* Mary's heart screamed.

When Daddy noticed her, he came running too. He grabbed her and pinned her to him. She had always turned to him for comfort and understanding. Now she punched his chest and kicked to get away.

"Mary! Mary! Why were you there? Didn't your mother tell you I would be back in time for dinner? Mary! Mary! Talk to me!"

Absolutely infuriated, she fought for words. He who had taught her to love the creatures of the earth. Was it all a lie? Some cute story to tell a little girl? "Why, Daddy? Why?"

"Why the hunt? Your uncle needs the meat for his family. He doesn't have the money to run to the store for food like we do. Most of his food he grows or hunts. You've seen his garden, the jars of food Aunt Ginny puts up. They need meat too."

"But to kill that incredible creature?"

"You eat animals every day, Mary. What about the hamburger we got on the way up here? And I do believe chicken is your favorite. They too are incredible creatures, aren't they?"

"I guess so, but at least I don't have to see them being killed."

"You didn't have to see this either, did you? You're the one who brought yourself out here. Maybe before you insist on your way you should be sure you are strong enough to handle it."

"You always helped me before, Daddy."

"I'm helping you now, Mary. Don't be too slow to know it!" He turned toward the house, not hesitating a moment to see if she would follow. He had work to do, and he was going to help his brothers. His attitude called on her to shape up and do the same.

With head bowed, Mary slowly followed her father out of the woods. After only a few steps, the heat of the day hit her face, and she looked up, surprised to see how close they had been to the house. When with leaden feet she made it back, she noticed the men as they worked hard getting the deer meat finished. The afternoon was hot and the smell of blood new to her. Mama kept trying to get her to come away from it all.

After a while, Mary's grandmother came outside and told the men to hurry up. The sound of the dinner bell could be heard for miles around as Grandma rang over and over, calling the family to come to the table. Mama had to pull Mary by the arm to get her inside the house to set the tables. The meal was a favorite: fried chicken, sweet milk gravy, potatoes piled and dripping with butter, green beans, and melt-in-your-mouth yeast rolls. Mary couldn't help but wonder if the hen she had seen walking around the yard was the same one now fried up for dinner. She tried not to think about the animals as she took her place beside Cal.

The room filled with people, and Mary was never sure exactly who they were. Later she learned that Daddy was one of twelve children. The whole family had made it a point to come home that day to visit. One of Mary's favorite relatives turned out to be Daddy's niece. She was older than he was, but as an infant, she had simultaneously contracted several diseases, leaving her mind equal to that of a five-year-old child. She was happy and fun loving, and Mary was proud of the way the family treated her. She felt such a part of the group, but there was one dissenter. Mama sat in a chair away from the table. When Daddy went over to encourage her to join everyone, she instead kept going over the horrible day. She gave Daddy no rest. "Something horrible is going to happen here. There are too many guns and too many people. You brought us here when I begged you to stay away from these people," Mama said. Mary listened while other voices in the room stilled. It broke her heart to hear the words. Mama would win. She always did.

After supper, most of Daddy's brothers and sisters returned home and the rest settled in and got ready for bed. Grandmother came in to give Mary an extra kiss and lovingly patted her face. As she left, she turned on several night-lights. Sprawled out in bed, Mary wondered what events the next day would bring. Sadly, she didn't have to wait until morning to learn why

Mama insisted years ago that Daddy should leave his people and make his home with her.

Several popping sounds punctuated the night. Mary wasn't sure if the sound was in her head or had really happened. She reasoned she must have been dreaming about the hunt earlier in the day. Struggling from her slumber, she listened to what sounded like some sort of strange humming. Where was it coming from? Mary decided it was more a type of moaning. She moved cautiously into the living room. In the semidarkness, she could barely make out her cousin sitting on the floor. The girl appeared to be rocking someone back and forth. In the faint light, Mary couldn't figure out what was going on. As she moved closer, her bare feet recoiled from some sticky substance that rapidly moved across the floor. She recognized a smell. It was the smell of blood accompanied by another odor. Mary coughed as smoke filled her nostrils. As she stood there, her Uncle Sam staggered into the room apologizing for firing his gun in the house. Mary remembered him saying something about trying to clean it and it going off.

In the same instant that the room blazed with light, Mary knew what had happened. Her poor slowwitted cousin sat on the floor hugging her father's body. Not understanding why he wouldn't wake up, she kept trying to get him to talk to her. Mary had yet to realize that it was his blood that had spread across the room and reached up like bony fingers to soak her nightgown. Timidly she walked over and knelt on the floor beside the confused girl. Gently, she took shaking arms away from the body. Laying him on the floor, Mary began to cradle her cousin, and they rocked together. Moans turned to wailing when the rest of the family fumbled into the room.

They stood there and stared. Maybe Mama had been right about them. Maybe they were too used to the sound of guns. Mary sat there waiting for some grown-up to take charge, to fix the awful mess. Instead time was as suspended as a broken tree limb after a summer storm. She wondered what they thought.

Finally, Mary could stand it no longer. "Please help us. Can't someone clean this girl up?" she begged. Trying to stand, she realized she couldn't. Fear had taken hold of her legs. Nothing in her world had prepared her for the face of death, and judging from the expressions on the faces in the room, it was a lesson that, if taught, is never learned.

Mama's screams broke the spell. Her face a twisted mask of agony, she glared at Daddy. "You promised me. Look what you've brought to the child. We were never to come to this place."

Mary didn't remember leaving that night. Mama and Daddy never spoke of it, and, in time, she wondered if it had been some sort of nightmare. One night she bravely searched the house for her favorite nightgown. She never found it. For a time, Daddy acted as if he needed to pay a daily penance, and their closeness was the price. Mama now had the excuse to pull Mary deeper into her world and Mary had the excuse to let her.

Several weeks after visiting Daddy's family, soft voices could be heard talking late into the night. Usually the sound of Mama and Daddy talking brought comfort. Mary couldn't understand their words, but the melodious drone of their conversation would lull her safely into slumber. This night, however, brought something different to her heart. Worried and wakeful, Mary needed to be with somebody. Mama had come into her bedroom several times and insisted she stay in bed. "Mary, pull your covers up and think of something pretty till you go to sleep. Try," she pleaded. "Daddy and I need to talk."

Mary did try, but it was useless. She grabbed a book, but her active mind wouldn't stop thinking back to the night spent with Daddy's family. Her cousin's face drifted across her memory every time she closed her eyes. Mary felt that the poor woman-child would probably never be told exactly what had happened. No one would tell her because people assumed she couldn't understand. Mary so wished she could talk to her and believed she could have been helpful. Mary had discovered the girl was a lot sharper than most people realized. Not a single tiny bug or flying bird had escaped her notice. And what intrigued Mary the most was that creatures noticed her. It was like there was some shared sweet communion. Mary, who heartily bragged about her way with animals, was completely outdone by this simpleton. It wasn't that her cousin was too dumb to be afraid like most of the aunts claimed. It was that she shared their spirit. They knew they would be taken care of by the Father and so did she. Maybe that knowledge was what separated children from adults. Mary guessed that when you were grown-up and had so much on your mind it was easy to forget the things the angels put into your heart.

That night the sound of parental voices drove Mary crazy. She decided to creep closer, so she inched her way silently up the hall. Pulling a pillow with her, she positioned herself on her stomach with her head barely poking around the door frame. She heard someone sniffle, like they were holding back tears. It couldn't be Mama. When Mama cried, she was so loud that the whole community knew it. Mary slid across the hardwood floor for a better view. Her heart felt a sharp stab of pain from what she witnessed. Her dear, sweet daddy had turned away from the window. As he did, a single tear slid down his face and dropped off his chin onto the nothingness of the bare floor. His shoulders were slumped as if a great weight had fallen upon them. He leaned over and kissed Mama's forehead and then went out the other door of their room and into the bathroom. Mama slowly moved toward the window and looked out to the coming morning. She appeared to be immensely tired, and her face looked old in the light of day. Even the house seemed heavy with a great sadness. The family moved under a dark cloud.

Mary went back to bed and prayed to the God of her teachings. Flopping onto her tummy, she felt a hand slowly rub her back. It was a huge hand, but its gentle touch soothed. "God, what does all this mean?"

Mary asked, surprised at the sound of her own voice. Somehow she knew she would never see Daddy's people again, but to see the pain it caused him made her feel battered too. Strange how Mama was equally sad. They needed a soulful day, and Mary wished she knew how to help her parents. She thought a picnic might help. She knew that Daddy would perk up if she could get him outside.

Her ideas were washed away with the rain that came pouring down after breakfast. Daddy sat in his chair with a paper in front of his face pretending he was alone, and Mama stayed in the kitchen making too much lunch food and a sour cream pound cake. Mary was not invited into either realm.

At her wit's end to stop the tension, Mary thought about lying on the floor and kicking and screaming like a two-year-old. Her mind begged for some Almighty help when the winds picked up and the power went out. At least for a little while, there would be no more paper reading or cooking.

"We need to take cover. The storm is getting rough," Mama said.

Daddy walked toward a window. "I think we should open the doors and enjoy the storm."

They settled for sitting together, somewhat away from the window, and listening to the wind sing. Mama wasn't too thrilled with the idea at first, but she soon moved into the circle of Daddy's arms. They were quiet and still. The weather stormed about them with a fury, and they were not afraid.

No Reservations

Mary dozed; they all did. The sound of the storm was gone, and it was the quiet of its leaving that woke her. The world was washed clean; so too their hearts.

"Can you see out the window, Mary?"

"Yes, Daddy. Why?"

"Want to test me? I'll close my eyes and listen really hard, and then I'll tell you the kinds of birds I hear."

"Birds?" Mary stretched. "Okay, if you want to."

"I'm trying to listen. Be really quiet now." His eyes twinkled merrily at Mama. "Okay, do you hear that pretty song? It's kind of shrill? It's a redbird, and it's the daddy calling for his mate after the storm."

Mary got up to peek out the window. "Hey, you're right about the redbird. I see it. But how do you know it's the daddy?"

"It's called a cardinal, Mary, and the daddy bird is the biggest and the brightest in color. The mama bird has a little more brown on her."

"Yeah! I think I see the mama now! Look. They do seem to be talking to each other."

"Told you! Do you see the little robin bird? She has a red chest. Watch her go up to her nest in that maple tree there."

"Yes, I do see her. How'd you know that her nest was in there?"

"It's been there a couple of years. The robin builds a clay bottom nest and puts new grass in it each year. I've watched her awhile now."

Mama spoke up then, playfully poking Daddy in the ribs. "Now wait just a minute here, you two. I think

I was the one who first noticed that little lady working on her nest."

"How do you know this? Are you making this up?"

Mama and Daddy both giggled as they exchanged looks of conspiracy.

Daddy said, "Now, Mary, would we tease you?"

"How do you know it?" she insisted.

"From living, princess. Look around, see things, notice, and remember. Just from living."

The family sat for a time enjoying the feel of being close to each other. Each knew they had to move on together, bearing whatever pain that life sent along. Mary would waste too much of her life searching for answers that were unimportant. The question "Why?" would haunt her for decades. She would forever doubt what she was blessed with. Having been placed in the security of a loving home would save her time and again. She would fight against the good of knowing she had a place she could always come back to and be sure.

10

After all the heartache their families had dished out, Mama and Daddy needed the help and comfort of a higher spirit. Mary's knowledge of religion was composed from what she was taught at church. Mama held firm to the belief that it was her duty to train her child in the way she should go.

"Mary, go tell your father we need to leave."

Mary looked out the window and saw him digging in the garden. "I don't think he's ready."

"Go out there and tell that man we're leaving. I'm tired of waiting on him."

Mary watched him walk up to the house. "He's coming, Mama."

Her mother met him at the door. "Why aren't you ready?"

"I'll change and be there shortly. It's a pretty day. I don't see why we have to be at church every time the doors open."

A frown drew Mama's brows together. "Something about a promise," she said.

Daddy sighed. "I'll be there," he said.

Mary suppressed a giggle as she and Mama got in the car. Sometimes she knew he came late on purpose, and Mary couldn't figure out what he did while she and Mama were at Sunday school. For a short time, Daddy had taught the children's class. The older members put a stop to that as soon as they found out he held class outside. Losing his little class hurt his feelings. Even so, he continued to do a lot of work at church. Many in the congregation found themselves inspired by his dedication. Over time most of the disapproving ones passed. In the community as well as at church, Daddy became more influential. He had a quiet presence, like the calm still of night, that appealed to people. Mary noticed that many sought his opinion. That ended one warm Easter Day when Daddy caused what Mama referred to as "the big explosion." It rocked their home as well as the community.

Easter morning dawned bright and clear that year. The Easter bunny left goodies hidden around the house and in the yard. Though she was too old to believe in such nonsense, Mama insisted she play along, and Mary was pleased to find a pair of snow-white gloves in her basket. A sweet smell surrounded her as Mama put flowers in her hair. The gloves, tight and smooth, made her feel grown-up. It was a good feeling to march into church that morning. Slowly Mary was accepted into her mother's world. When Mama reached over and gave her hand a gentle squeeze, she felt complete. She wanted to be a part of her mother's life, a part of anything that offered a constant connection.

Daddy was on time that day but didn't sit down because he was an usher. He stood at the door, welcomed everyone, and helped visitors find seats. There was an audible sigh when he escorted a black family to a pew close to the front. Mary had the oddest feeling that even the family felt a little disturbed by this. As the sermon began, she watched the people around her and soon realized that they weren't paying much attention to the preacher. She could tell that most of the congregation found the black family's presence very disturbing.

Mary tried to turn her attention back to the minister as he reached the high point of his sermon. "And I tell you on this Easter morning Jesus came alive for us! Each and every one of you sitting here today has a place in glory!" As the minister screamed those words, he gazed out upon the audience, pointing a finger for emphasis. His finger stopped on the black family, and he lost his place in his text. The hush became an almost tangible thing, and only the wail of a baby broke the silence.

When church was over, there wasn't the group of people who normally gathered around the door to chat. Mama's warmth toward Mary had turned sour. She placed her hand roughly on the girl's shoulder and pushed her to the car.

"Mary," she said softly, "be quiet. Hurry now. Get in the car." No other words had been uttered.

Daddy strode confidently toward his truck with an odd smile on his face. He waved at his girls. He seemed filled up that morning, happy. Mary sure hoped Mama would come around to his way of thinking by afternoon.

Finishing Sunday dinner, Mama cringed when a neighbor dropped by to invite Daddy back to church. Mama's strange noises made Mary think she was going to choke on her dessert. Daddy was gone a long time. Mama spent the whole while pacing the house, saying, "Oh no! Oh, no!" about to wear herself down.

The door burst open, and Daddy came in like a raging bull. Talking to no one in particular, he yelled, "I was told God loved— no, I think it was welcomed everyone. Is that everyone with white skin?" His tone softened like the calm before the storm. "Did you notice that I'm a little darker than most? I've made a lot of promises to you, lady, and here is one more. I'll never set foot in your church again!" With a slam of the door, he was gone, leaving Mama too stunned to cry.

Mary slipped outside and followed him to the woodpile. She wondered why Daddy thought he needed kindling chopped on such a hot day, but she soon realized that the anger flowed out with his sweat. When he finally stopped, he was able to give his best smile. He hugged her close and promised, "Next Sunday, I'll take you to my church, Mary. Then you will never wonder again where God is."

11

When next Sunday arrived, Mary didn't know what to expect. Daddy pulled out old shoes and blue jeans. "Get a jacket, Mary," he said.

Mama dressed for church as usual and lightly kissed Mary's forehead as she went out the door. She hadn't uttered a word to Daddy.

After Mama left, Mary got dressed as fast as she could. Not caring what the plan was, she decided to be pleased enough not to have to put on tight shoes and a prickly petticoat. Daddy drove north, up toward the mountains. For a while, Mary wondered if they were going back to his home place. After what felt like forever, he turned onto another road. They came upon what looked like some sort of starting place. It was a trail. Mary was confused and wondered what he had in mind. As they moved up the pathway, she saw a welcoming sign to the Appalachian Trail.

As they walked, Daddy cautioned, "Be careful to look around, Mary." He walked slowly, maintaining a steady pace and pointed out new blooms and wildlife along the way. "Mary, look." He gestured toward a beautiful white bloom. "That's mountain laurel. Isn't it pretty? Some people buy that I've heard. Wonder how they keep it alive in the city." He shook his head as if questioning himself. About halfway up the mountain, he stopped to look down at a lake. No words were necessary. Mary slipped her hand in his, feeling an intensity that almost moved her to tears.

Yes, this place belonged to her too. She felt the trees were glad to have them as visitors. Even the birds seemed to offer guidance up the mountain, flying back and forth as if encouraging them to adopt a faster pace. Mary could almost feel wings sprouting on her back, could almost feel her feet leaving the earth. Something was happening inside of her. A subtle change took hold, and she liked it. When they got to the top of the world, Mary felt strength fill her. Daddy's smile deepened when she turned to him. The sweet look on his face told her that she had discovered all that he wanted her to know.

Coming upon a large rock, they stopped to sit down to rest. Daddy pulled her into his lap and picked a single blade of grass. "You know, Mary, our Creator made this grass and everything else you can see. If you ever feel sad or lonely or not able to make a decision, you can always come to the woods to find Him." Daddy paused and looked deep into Mary's eyes. "And the greatest gift of all is when you see His face in the smiles of your children."

With that, they were silent. When the time came to go, each felt soothed by the morning together. Mary wondered when Mama would realize that the Spirit she was always searching for, Daddy had already found.

When they got home Mama was waiting with dinner. She moved around her kitchen calm and happy, not the least bothered by their day together. The whole family was trying to move on to a happier place. Sadly though, as they slowly grew closer together, the rest of the world reared its ugly head time and time again. It started so innocently that Mary was almost drawn into the hate herself. Cousin Dessie was getting married. Mama was all in a whirl. She was in charge of most everything and even made the wedding gown. Mama was so pleased with herself during those days. All the family praised her work, and she reacted like a tired little puppy that has someone rubbing its head behind the ears. All the warm, cozy feelings spilled over to everyone around. Even Daddy, who usually had no time for women stuff, joined the fun.

Treats for the table filled the refrigerator, the freezer, and every inch of counter space. Peeking inside huge plastic containers, Mary discovered what must have been a thousand tiny sandwiches cut in heart shapes, the crust neatly trimmed away. Melon balls in shades of pink, red, and green peeked from the freezer door. Flowers were carefully put in the back porch refrigerator. Opening the door was like pouring out bottles of fine perfume. Jars of nuts and bags of candy peeked from the corners. The skill of Mama's handiwork was amazing. Still, she seemed to need help with her tasks.

"Mary, can you get me the laundry basket?"

"Why? You gonna wash clothes?" Mary put her hands on her hips in what could only be perceived as a defiant stance. "I thought you needed to work on the wedding?"

"I am. I'm down to the last chores," Mama said as she dug in the top of a closet. "The only thing left to do is wash and press the tablecloths. Come go with me."

They packed the tablecloths and a blanket loaded then in the back of her father's truck and went around to the basement of one of the businesses up town. Mary had always wondered what was down there. Several washing machines were already going, and the dryers made it humid and warm. The door was propped open, probably as much for ease in carrying through a load as for comfort from the oppressive steam in the room. Nobody seemed very happy or willing to talk, so Mary sat by Mama and read an old magazine that had been left on the bench. After a while, she got bored and nosed around a bit. A sign on the door said, "White Only." It was scribbled in a childish scrawl. Mary wondered why it would only be allowed to wash white clothes. When Mama put the light blue blanket into the machine she tried to stop her and pointed to the sign.

"What is it, Mary?" Mama asked, rather frustrated.

"Maybe you shouldn't wash the blue blanket."

"What in the world are you talking about? That sign is talking about people, Mary."

"People! You mean you can only wash white people?" Suddenly, she understood the full extent of what she said and was horrified. "Is that why Daddy didn't come? Because he isn't white?" Before she had time to realize what she'd said, the sting of Mama's slap crossed her face.

"Why would you say something like that? Your Daddy is as white as we are. Sometimes you are the meanest person I have ever known."

From that day forward, Mary knew she would be expected to consider herself a little white girl. Despite the shock of Mama's temper, Mary wanted her to know that she understood. Still, she didn't know what to say to her or how to react. So she said nothing. Her face was hot where she had been hit, and she felt herself start to cry. Surely Mama hadn't meant to do that to me, Mary tried to convince herself. With sudden clarity, she realized, as she noticed everyone staring, that Mama was not one bit sorry she had struck her child, only sorry that someone had seen.

Thankfully the laundry was soon finished. They gathered each piece and returned to the car in silence. Mary had so much going on in her head that she felt exhausted. She wanted to shut it out. When they got to the church, the bustle of preparation was a welcomed distraction.

Mama put out the clean cloths and the borrowed table settings. She had two huge punch bowls, one on each side of the room. Roses were everywhere, producing an almost overpowering sweet fragrance. Little mints filled candy bowls, and bags of rice wrapped up in satin rested prettily around each dish. It was the most beautiful thing Mary had ever seen. The memory of earlier events pushed their way back into her mind. The room, made ready for a bridal party, seemed the absolute opposite of the ugly she had witnessed a few scant hours before.

When the church finally passed inspection, Mama and Mary went home to ready themselves. Mama was silent and moody. Mary wondered if she were nervous, like the bride, or angry because of what had happened earlier. She took special care to dress and put up her hair the way Mama liked. It didn't matter. Mama took no notice of any attempts to pacify.

Mama retreated to her bedroom for a while and came out dressed in a navy blue dress. The blue complimented her, but it was too dark for a wedding. Even so, Daddy gave a loud whistle as she entered the living room in search of her lipstick. She met his attempts at play with an angry glare. Daddy and Mary bowed their heads, as if in shame, at her reproach and went outside to wait for her to be ready.

An hour later, Mary proudly entered the church on her daddy's arm. Mama was somewhere crying with the bride. She had planned to sit up front to direct the service. As Mary and her father moved up the aisle toward the front pews, white-gloved hands reached out to pat her face and perfumed necks pressed their essence against her skin. She was forced to stop over and over again to greet Mama's friends. She began to feel almost as if she were the bride. *Why couldn't life always move in such beauty and grace?* Mary wondered. The celebrations of times glorious were too few and much too fragile.

Noises from the back of the church interrupted her lofty thoughts. The music swelled. Guests stood in honor of what appeared to be an angel gliding down the aisle. As she faced her followers, Mary found herself gasping at the beauty.

As the couple exchanged vows, Mary couldn't help remembering her parents' story. Daddy had decided never to contact his family again. None would speak of it. It was over for eternity. *Why does Mama ask so much of him*, Mary pondered, *and why does he gladly give it?* She searched his face for a glimmer of regret of his vows of love. There was nothing there except a shy smile. She wondered if, as he sat there, he thought about his beloved. Mary knew he was proud of her then, and he was proud of her now. His eyes sparkled as he noticed her across the room. A silent message passed between them carried by a slight nod only they understood.

That night, tossing and tumbling in bed, it should have been easy to fill a youthful mind with the beauty of the close of day. Mary ought to have been able to relive the moments soaking in the goodness. Instead, her thoughts traveled back to the past. She wished she understood what knowledge she was supposed to gain from all that went on in the world. How much would be too much?

12

Mama and Mary went to the grocery store a couple of weeks later. The parking lot was laid out so that when you parked your car it was nose to nose with somebody else's. While Mama paid for the groceries; Mary hurried out ahead of her. She noticed a pretty colored lady who had a small child riding on the bottom of her buggy, another one riding in her buggy, and a baby in her arms. As she cut across to her car, another car slowly began to move toward her. Unaware of the threat, she juggled her children as she tried to find her keys. Mary guessed she didn't sense her trouble until it was almost too late. When she looked up, the car had moved in like a shark sniffing blood. Ever so quietly she and her children had become pinned up against another auto. A maniacal laugh from the car's white driver ripped through the air. The woman's face showed no fear, and that seemed to encourage the man.

"Hey, honey, you need some help with that load?" The laugh sounded again, making Mary cringe. "Darling, how many babies ya got thar?" he asked as he leaned out the window of his car. "Need another man to lighten 'em up a bit? Maybe you'd rather mate with a monkey?" Opening his door, he started to get out. "That least one got some mighty funny-looking ears."

Calmly she shifted her youngest in her arms, instructed the other two to grab each side of her skirt, left her buggy, and moved toward her car. The white man got out and pretended he wanted to help carry her bags.

"Hey, darling, it ain't polite to ignore somebody that's trying to help you." Mary watched him pick up each of her bags. He then dropped them one by one onto the hard-paved parking lot. "Oh my goodness, I think I must have grease on my hands. Hey, come here woman. See if I can rub some in your hair. Hey, don't you hear?" He scratched himself and got back in his car. He drove over her entire load, tires squealing as he left the lot.

Too shocked to move, Mary watched her salvage what she could. She found herself praying the man would end up with a flat tire from the glass he had shattered. *Has this kind of evil always existed?* she wondered. Had she never noticed? Mary had convinced herself the "White Only" sign that was hastily scribbled and taped to the wall of the washroom was some sort of joke. It was impossible for her to believe the sign actually referred to other people. She had studied about the civil rights movement in school. Scenes of violence that were flashed across the television screen came back to her mind. Those struggles had brought about change. And yet, here today, Mary had witnessed a single act that was so repugnant to her that she felt physically ill. Turning, she realized that Mama had come out sometime during the incident. Mary watched as Mama matter-of-factly loaded up the groceries into the car and climbed behind the steering wheel. Disturbed, Mary stared for only a moment at all those who had witnessed the scene. She took note of her mama's cool composure. Her heart tore at her brain as she slid into the car, trying to reconcile her thoughts and emotions. No matter what Mama said, she and daddy were obviously darker than most of the people she knew.

"Mama."

"Hush, Mary."

"Did you see that man? Did you see what he did?"

Mama's eyes bored into the rearview mirror as she backed out of her space. She turned the steering wheel with exaggerated movements as if the act required her total concentration.

"Mama, did you ..."

"I said, hush." Mama smiled and waved at a neighbor that was standing on the sidewalk. The woman nodded in return. It was to be a normal day.

Mary crossed her arms over her chest. The darkness wasn't just a skin color, she decided. It was a darkness that permeated the fairest, most righteous face. She couldn't grasp the importance of what she'd seen, only that she had to push it away.

She vowed not to return to town. She would simply stay in her hideout and enjoy the beauty of the small yard. She could read about a delightful delicacy or a faraway place. She could surround herself with dreams, beautiful stories, and grand ideas.

Mary thought of the stories of Peter Pan. Sadly, she realized that he was only someone else hoping as she hoped. Grandmother once teased, saying, "You'll grow up, like it or not!" How right she was.

13

Days linger when you are a child. As Mary rambled through her fenced yard, each hour seemed to float into the next until she couldn't remember what day it was. After almost deciding that summer would ever end, the coolness of fall brought a change to the world. Everyone moved with smiles blown about like the falling leaves. Sleeves rolled up during the summer heat were turned down. The old ones reached for comforting coats and long underwear to nestle themselves in warmth.

Relief from the heat softened Mama. For some reason, unknown to everyone, Mary was suddenly deemed old enough to be allowed out of the gated boundaries. Giddy with newfound freedom, she chose to climb over the chain-link fence instead of taking advantage of gates that gaped open like the smile of a young child who has lost a first tooth. Mary thought herself a princess free to chase wishes farther and farther out into the realm. She hardly noticed Daddy coming out of the house to watch her escape. He laughed as she hoisted herself over the pointed edges along the top of the fence. For a moment, the gate grabbed Mary's pants and she thought she wouldn't make it.

"Hey there, little girl," Daddy called. "Why don't you use the gate? Be a lot better on your britches."

Mary chose to ignore his taunts. With a sudden surge of independence, she pulled free. Never stopping to look back or wonder about any danger that her choice could bring, she plowed through the underbrush. The woods called to her and promised refuge from the hated world that had been discovered in the summer sun. Mary pushed to forget the ravings of man and the anger that threatened to control.

Proceeding deeper into the cool of the woods, her father became a distant blur among the cornstalks he was trying to tie. A muted conversation could be heard across the winds as he praised the corn and hoped for another fine crop in the future. A soft mist started to fall, and Mary became lost in the mixed perceptions of a dream. Her senses quickened, and she reached out her tongue to taste the thick droplets dissolving into the world around her. Ears, pricked like the wolf, listened for the sounds of the birds. Her head tilted, hearing the songs and cataloging the birds as she remembered each melody, forgetting who had taught her the tune. Stepping slowly heel to toe, she meticulously missed the few still dry leaves and moved silently across the land.

Mary had no knowledge of why she was sneaking down the hill, where she was going, or what drove her. Daddy informed her long ago that water ran down. She knew she wouldn't find much more than a spring on top of the mountain. Still, she remembered that there was a lake nearby. Little drips of water that would become a creek invited Mary to follow. She obliged, hoping to find a welcome spot to rest and seek her solace. Not to be disappointed, Mary gasped with delight as the clouds of the stormy morning pulled themselves back as if a giant curtain had opened up to a glorious stage.

In disbelief, she realized she had been here before. *I recognize it now*, she thought to herself. The lake was really a wide part of the river, and she had played on other banks. She remembered imagining herself walking through the woods on her way back from school. As the school bus jostled along, she had often pretended she was sitting on the sunny bank, dressed in soft cotton and lace, watching the fish jump. Mary prided herself on being the first to notice the early flowers in spring. Until now, she had had to settle for picking the little wild ones by the driveway. This day the woods gave up their bounty of mountain laurel and ferns. Mary's soul sparkled as she followed the road of her imaginings.

After the path ran out, wandering legs had to make way through the brambles. Pleased to come to a small clearing, she stood looking across at the same spot that, in the last days of spring, could barely be seen out of the bus windows. The water drew her closer as if some spirit was calling, calling her gently to the shore. Mary pulled her damp jacket close about her body, fighting the urge to shiver. The water danced over smooth rocks, mesmerizing her with a sound that resounded in the mind like an ancient song. She stayed far too long enjoying the magic the surroundings produced in her mind and in her heart.

As night descended, she realized Mama and Daddy would be furious with her for being out so late. Daddy trusted her as she had left the confines to explore that morning. Mary knew better than to betray that trust. She purposely hadn't mentioned going down to the river. Mama was terrified of water, so Mary was usually very careful not to get too close to even a tiny puddle.

As darkness swiftly fell about her, she noticed a light glowing near the bank. The comforting trees had become full of shadows in the dissipating light. Mary had no idea where she was. Her ignorant movements had left her with no sense of direction, no idea how to get home. Oddly, she was unafraid. She crept closer to the light.

Without warning, Daddy's voice sounded almost at her ear. It startled Mary so badly that she fell, skidded down the bank, and landed right in the middle of the stream.

"Now you've done it, little girl. I'll never be able to convince your mama that you didn't play in the water."

"Daddy, how long have you been there? You nearly scared me to death!"

"You should learn to be more watchful if you intend to go traipsing off by yourself. You not only missed my signs but also most of the ones the land tried to give you. Haven't you recognized where you are yet?"

Squinting, trying to look through the last prisms of light, Mary stared in amazement at the back of their yard. Could that be her favorite childhood hideout taunting her through the night sky? Vines almost covered the old board. She had managed to bring herself almost back home without even realizing it.

The distant corner of the fence winked at her. Why had she never noticed how close the stream was to the house? Was it because the yard was completely fenced in and she had never ventured out? Did the trees, vines, and grasses hide this place completely? Mary felt giddy with newfound power. She could climb the fence and be here in an instant. Funny, you live somewhere all your life and never look around to see where you really could be.

Daddy once again interrupted her thoughts. "Mary, are you ready to get home to supper now? Mama was starting to worry, so she sent me looking. I heard you headed this way. Did you enjoy your little trek?"

"Yeah. Daddy, what is that glowing stuff around the river bank?"

"That's what the fairy queen left to guide her stray little fairies home."

"Oh, Daddy! Can we walk the long way home? I need the night a little longer."

"You need the night? I think your mama needs you, little lady. What is it you think you'll see?"

"I don't know, Daddy. I feel something here. Whose land is this anyway?"

"This is my land, Mary."

"Daddy, no! You should have included it inside the fence. You mean I can walk it anytime?"

"Well, not anytime. I don't want you to get hurt out here. I have some friends who come here sometimes to camp and what not."

"I saw a ring of rocks and thought it looked like it had been a campfire. You let your friends come out here? Why?"

"You said yourself it felt good to be here. I couldn't fence the river, Mary, so I just try to keep track of who comes around. Just in case."

"In case of what, Daddy?"

"I guess in case there's some problem here. Come on, Mary. Your mama will be mad at both of us if we don't hurry it up. I'll bring you out here another time maybe."

"When? Do we need to pick a time when Mama won't know?"

Daddy stopped walking and turned to face her. Though the darkness shielded his features, Mary was sure he wasn't pleased. For a moment, his stance made her regret all the questions. She didn't mean to hurt him, but he knew things that she needed to know. He had held things back from her all her life, and she was getting tired of it. As they trudged back to the house, Mary vowed to herself that she would surely hold him to his promise of return.

Deciding it would be a good idea to try to stay on Mama's good side, Mary worked hard to please. Keeping Mama happy had its advantages. She thought doing her chores without being asked would show Daddy that he could trust her and prayed it would urge him to make good on his promise to take her back into his woods. It wasn't working. Mama was restless.

Late one night Mary heard her parents talking. Her mother seemed to be struggling. She wanted Daddy's permission to make a decision. Mary supposed he wasn't listening much since she could hear the rustle of the newspaper. Later she heard crying and wished she knew what was so hard on her mama. Whatever it was, Mama decided the only person who would understand her was her mother and soon made plans for a visit to Grandma's that would not include Daddy.

When Mama and Mary got to Grandma's, the women made their way into the back bedroom. The air was cool and smelled of the sweet cedar that the wardrobe in the corner was made of. Mary was privileged to be allowed to listen to their talk. She guessed that for some reason unknown to her she had somehow earned the right to be part of the women. The emotional power in the room amazed. It quickly became obvious that Mama had already made her choice, but she just kept asking permission from everybody. She so needed to hear that it was okay to do something for herself.

"I've decided I want to go to college and earn a degree so I can work in an elementary school. I want to help children learn to love books the way I do." Mary was proud of Mama as she talked.

Grandmama didn't seem the least bit shocked by this declaration. "Well, I have a little nest egg tucked away that your papa doesn't know about. You can have all of it if you need it."

"Oh, Mama, then it's not selfish of me to go back to work? Mary is in school all day anyway. She's old enough to come home by herself. Our schedules would almost be the same. I can take classes during the day while she's at school, and she wouldn't even know I was gone. Everybody I know thinks I'm crazy for doing this. I worked so hard to get Mary, and now I feel like I'm abandoning her."

"Now, dear, you know you can make a difference for the better in this small part of the world. Think about all the teachers in the family." Grandmama settled back onto the feather mattress. "It's natural for you to want to teach. Someday Mary will know what a great gift your determination is, if she doesn't know already."

"Oh, Mama, I would never do anything to take me away from Mary! She's my life, but I know there's more for me."

Mary decided they had forgotten her. She sat on the other side of the bed and listened, her solitaire game forgotten. She had never heard her mama put into words how important she was to her. Mary basked in a warm glow, knowing that although she planned to do something for herself, Mama would never sacrifice her child's needs. At that moment, she too decided to one day become a teacher.

After classes started, Mama would work late into the night to get her homework done. Mary would still have homemade cookies in the afternoon, Girl Scout patches beautifully sewn in place, and a list of chores waiting for her. Often Mary would wonder how Mama found the strength to keep life normal. She overheard her mama actually ask permission of Daddy when her final exams altered her schedule and he had to be responsible for an extra two hours.

Mama left their meals prepared, and, after they ate, they left the dishes for her to put away when she got home. Her decision was major, life altering, and never never easy, but even as she worked so hard to keep it from affecting Mary, she didn't seem to realize her choice was a lesson that went into making a restless child into a caring woman.

Mary soon began to feel her absence even when Mama tried so hard to save her from it. Everything in the house was tiptop, but she wasn't there. The smell of her rose perfume didn't linger like it used to. Often Mary had to walk home to a friend's house instead of her own. She found herself missing her mama's silly smile and the permanent question, "How was your day, dear?" Through the years Mary had gotten used to not answering, but she could never welcome not being asked. She began to realize it was her mother's very presence, much as it sometimes bothered her, that made life comfortable, secure, and stable.

14

Late one Saturday morning, Mary came home from a party with friends. Mama was in the garden gathering vegetables. Sweat dripped from her face. She always wore an apron, and she always had a tissue. Sometimes it chased a runny nose; sometimes it wiped the grime of the day's toil. Mary joined Mama in the vegetable gathering and then helped pile it all on the picnic table. As they worked, they chatted—the type of banter that fills the time. Usually Mama chose to work inside, but that day they sat down in the grass and began to break the beans.

"Mary, slow down, honey. Nobody wants to eat beans with those strings and tips left on them."

"Mama, do you ever think you're too picky?"

"Maybe, but you're the very one who puts a scowl on your face and pulls those tough strings off when we sit down at the table."

"Oh, Mama, I do not!"

Smiling lightly, she responded, "Besides, it doesn't take but a minute to pull the string down like this. You need to start on the right end of the bean." Carefully she adjusted that one bean until the fraying strings were gone and each break produced a perfect length.

"Mama, don't you ever get tired of this?"

"Why, what do you mean, dear?"

"Don't you ever want to throw the dumb bean in the pot whole or leave the beds unmade or jump in the car and drive until nobody can find you?"

"Well, yes, dear. You know going back to school has been fun for me. It gave me a chance to explore a new part of myself. I suppose that's what all the women libbers are trying to get us to do. But I still have to do all my other work too. Is that what you mean?"

"Maybe, but doesn't it make you mad that you still have all this other stuff to do when you get back home?"

"I suppose people want it to, but I have never been afraid of work. I cut my teeth on it. It's when I see people who have it all handed to them, who never have the opportunity to learn their own value..." She paused and seemed to sigh. "That's what makes me mad ... and afraid."

"Afraid?"

"Mary, I know you always get tired of me telling you, 'If it's worth doing, it's worth doing right.' I guess it does seem like a dumb way of thinking, but it worked for me. It makes a person feel good inside when they know they've done a job well. Your daddy has always lived by that too. These days I see so many people your age and they already have it all. What else can life bring them? They're all searching for themselves or some such silly notion. How can you lose yourself anyway? If you've got something to do, then you have something to feel important about, even if it's just a string bean. Oh, forget it. I don't know what I'm saying. Never mind about it anyway."

Mama had never talked to Mary like that before. Mary looked closely at the familiar face. *Find yourself,* she thought. *I understand the feeling. I don't know who I am.*

Mama groaned and stood up. "Get that bucket, will you?"

"Yes, Mama." Mary noticed a small sample of vegetables inside.

"Not enough of anything left to put up by itself." Mary smiled.

At the end of summer a big pot simmered on the stove. Tomatoes were always plentiful. Mama cut the last bit of corn, potatoes, carrots, and added whatever beans were available to the brew. Hours later, when a unique aroma filled the house, Mama deemed it soup and moved the pot to a table to cool. Sometime in the night Mary would hear sounds from the kitchen. She knew Mama carefully measured the precious mix into plastic bags and boxes. Vegetable soup would line one side of the freezer waiting for the cold winter months when it would be pulled out and served with hot cornbread. Daddy called it poor man's stew as he ate bowl after bowl, dipping the bread, and smacking like a hungry wolf.

Making soup, Mama?"

"That time of year, she answered.

"Another chore so you have a purpose?"

"It's another opportunity to do something worthwhile for my family, Mary. You won't understand it until you're older. Until you're a mother." She offered a weak smile. Peering in the bucket she evaluated the mix. "I'll start later on this. How about a sandwich?"

"For supper? Daddy won't care for that, will he?"

Mama sighed. "He's camping out with some friend tonight so it's just you and me."

Mary felt a strange shiver pass through her body. "Daddy isn't coming home?"

"Not tonight," Mama said, and offered Mary a stern look. "Probably not until late tomorrow. We'll go to church without him."

It was on the tip of Mary's tongue to say they now always went without him. Instead she pulled the vegetables from the bucket and began to wash them.

"Thank you, Mary." Mama said.

Mary nodded not sure if Mama thanked her for her help or her silence.

15

Sunday came and went. Daddy did not return. Mama woke Mary for school on Monday. The talk at breakfast was as dry as the toast.

"Mama, where is ..."

"I'm going to have to leave you and Daddy some supper. I've to stay late at school tonight.'

"He's coming home, isn't he?"

Mama cleared the table. "Of course he's coming home. Why wouldn't he come home? I told you he was with some friends. You might be home a while by yourself this afternoon."

"Alone?"

Mama kissed the top of her head. "Don't worry. He's not far away. Now, get a move on. You'll miss the bus."

Mary slowly walked out the door, turning often to look at Mama. She saw her leave the kitchen. Mary crept along the house. Through the front window, Mary watched Mama walk to the back of the house. The bus came chugging up the hill. Mary hid behind a bush and prayed. "You don't see me. Move on along."

Her prayers answered, Mary tried to still her breath. *Mama would find out. She'd probably get a phone call in the next thirty minutes.* A sudden noise frightened Mary. A sudden touch nearly stilled her heart. Cat slunk out of the bush with a squirrel in his mouth. He dropped his present in Mary's lap.

"Oh, what have you done?"

Cat began to yowl and to rub against her shoulder. He nudged the squirrel as if asking for approval.

Mary felt all the strength leave her body. The sound of the car starting felt like an assault. Cat purred and squatted in her lap. "She's leaving. Cat, she's leaving. She won't find out. At least not today."

Mary didn't know exactly what to do with herself. She grabbed Cat and went back in the house. She noticed Mama had tidied things up and left a snack on the counter. "Now, don't you think about getting into that," she warned. "That squirrel was enough mischief for you."

Cat snuggled closer, his head rubbing her chin, his purr growing louder.

"Come on you rotten thing. Let's go back to sleep for a while. Then we'll figure out what to do."

Morning turned to afternoon with a swiftness of time that astonished Mary. She'd slept for hours and spent the rest of the day reading. Cat seemed content to be her partner in crime. The sound of Daddy's truck pulling in the driveway struck terror in her heart.

"I'm caught," she whispered. "I'm caught and gonna be in such trouble."

She listened for Daddy to come in the house. He didn't. She peeked past her bedroom curtains for a sign of him. There was none.

"Something is not right. Mama's gone to class and Daddy is just gone." She glanced at Cat for courage. "Time for me to go hunting, I think." She stole out the back door to the porch. It was much later than she imagined. Darkness lingered on the edges of the day.

Deciding she knew where Daddy must be, she grabbed a flashlight and wandered out to the river path she'd recently discovered. Carelessly she tossed about the beam. About to give up any hope of finding her father, the sound of voices floated across the evening. Out of the darkness, Daddy appeared, put a finger to his lips to caution her silence, and led her around the gate to the stream and the supposed interlopers.

A shrill whistle that had always been Mary's call burst across Daddy's lips. She was startled to realize the sound was not meant for her. Someone in the group returned his call. Mary bent and peered through the darkness, finally seeing the flicker of a campfire. Entering the circle like the local royalty, Mary was astonished as everyone rose to greet her father. The group was a strange lot in Mary's eyes. She recognized a few men that most of the town considered misfits. *Mama would be in a rage if she knew Daddy had allowed me to partake in such a gathering*, Mary thought. Maybe it was the allure of the prohibited, maybe it was the pull of the ancients, maybe it was a need for a connection, but something made Mary feel that for that moment she was in a place that would afford a change in her being. She sat quietly by the campfire and listened to the stories. They were different from the ones read or told to her before in her life. Not parables exactly, yet important in their lessons to the people. An old man spoke, directing his imagery specifically to Mary. Quietly accepting his words was all that he required.

The hushed tones of the old man's voice soothed over a sad, disturbing story. "Man was given the earth by the Creator. He held dominion over the plants and the animals and was trusted to treat them fairly. He did not. He took much pleasure in the sport of killing the four-leggeds. He wasted their gifts. The animals took council to discuss man and his abuses. They decided to send him diseases to punish him for his acts against them. Man was smitten by terrible ravages of the body and of the mind. Over time the plants took pity over man and offered him medicine to combat the diseases sent him. Some men hear the voices of the immortals carried on the wind and take heed. Some still do not."

The stories Mary listened to that night jolted vague memories that seemed to float through her. She wondered how she was unable to discern between what she knew and what she had been told. An old woman approached her. They talked, but Mary couldn't remember how she knew her. The woman sat beside her, close, like a mother, and whispered, "Do not spend your time wondering about your parents or your people.

You learn in school all about who gave you your brown eyes and your bright smile. Genetics, I think you call it. Tonight you sit here wondering about what is inside. How do you know the things you know? It frightens you. Do you not know that the things that make up who you are carried on the blood? Why is that so hard to believe? You have the answers deep inside yourself. Let them out, little flower. Let them out."

Silently the darkness stole her away. Pensive, Mary settled back into Daddy's lap. Another whistle pierced in the night. Looking toward the sound, expecting to see a man's face, Mary gasped when out of the woods trotted a huge bear. Her body stiffened, but Daddy's lack of fear translated to her, and she forced herself to remain calm. The bear appeared to invite himself to their council. The appearance of his master offered some peace to Mary's wits. An irresistible force propelling her, she felt herself move nearer to the beast. She wanted, no had, to touch him. He wore an air of such dignity. She felt honored to be in his presence.

The group settled in, and the stories began to wind long. Sleep whispered the name of the younger ones. A calm like the fragile fog of morning wrapped itself around the gathering. The sound of a truck sliding, moving too fast disturbed the sweet kinship. A man bearded, huge, and smelly exited the vehicle. He was obviously drunk, even to a child's eyes, and this time it was Mary's Daddy who stiffened. Clarity of a new sort filled her mind. She realized that this idiot was a white man and that the people around her were not.

He came to them, loud and disrespectful. Mary hoped he would satisfy his curiosity and leave quickly. Her wish almost came true until he saw the bear.

The man circled the tame beast, making inane remarks. He jumped and threatened. He had some idiotic notion that the bear should fight him. He kept picking at the animal, popping his paws and trying to make him growl. The bear sat silent with the understanding of a father who patiently watches his son make a fool of himself. There was no torture that would force him to lose himself and fight back. Sadly, Mary's father did not have the same self-control.

Daddy was a small man, not someone who could easily defend even himself in a fight, and this would not be a fair one. The white man was large and full of the bully that all hate. Mary, thinking her presence would bring a measure of caution to him, tried to grab his arm. It might have worked had not the man chose that moment to pick up river sand and toss it into the bear's eyes. Still the gentle creature stood regal, but not Daddy. Full throttle he ran at the giant, knocked him back, and then jumped away before the bully could muster a swing. Finally the others held Daddy back and commanded peace. They put the drinker back in his truck and sent him on his way. The group dispersed quickly then, seemingly afraid of something. Daddy sat in an angry stupor until someone fairly ordered him to take his child's hand and get her to safety. Mary didn't know what could have possibly harmed them there in the woods, beside her river. It had been a happy place, and they were forced to flee it.

When they got home, Daddy put away the food she had forgotten to eat. Gruff, he said, "I think you'd better take your bath before your mother gets home."

Once scrubbed clean, she went straight to bed not so much to sleep as to think. Daddy came in to tuck her in. He was her normal father again and promised to send Mama in when she got home.

Mary lay in her bed and wondered about that night. The strangeness of the day almost overwhelmed her. The people on her land, the reaction to an intruder—all tore at her mind and her soul. *What is going on at the river? What causes such fear in the hearts of those gathered?*

Mary wondered about the people as they scattered. The ancient ones had faded, becoming merely one speck of time unto a day. One story passed to whom, and for what reason? Where were the old ones who knew the truth, danced the dance, and whispered a call to her heart.

The week passed with slow monotony. Each day Mary woke feeling more out of sorts than ever in her life. Thankful Saturday finally came, she pulled on her jeans and shirt, and walked out to her secret place. She wished for signs of her little squirrel friend but knew since Cat arrived he had moved on. "Everything moves on, I guess," she said to the wind. Climbing onto the board, she heard a crack. Something split and she barely made it to standing before the whole seat collasped. "Great. That's just terrific. Where will I find peace now?"

"Mary."

Daddy's voice sounded overloud and strained. "Mary, you out here?"

"Yes, Daddy."

He approached her. His face looked pale and strained. "Come inside, Mary."

"What's wrong?"

"We need to go to your Grandmama's house."

"It's Saturday. We go on Sunday."

"We need to go today."

Something sick grew in the pit of her stomach. She took a several tentative steps toward him and noticed Mama coming from the house. Her face was hard. She wore an expression Mary didn't recognize.

"Why? Why today?"

Mama wailed. "She's gone. My precious mother is gone."

"Gone?" Mary bit her tongue as the meaning of Mama's words sunk in. "She's dead?"

"Mary," Daddy said, "have some pity."

"Get in the house, both of you," Mama cried. "I've got things to do. I don't need you two around messing up the family business." Daddy nodded and gestured Mary toward the house. His shoulders slumped lower with every step. Mama pealed out of the driveway.

"Daddy, what do we do?"

"Your mother will let us know."

He used the word, mother. He's never said that about Mama. Mary followed her daddy until he sat down in his chair. Like magic the newspaper appeared in front of his face and she knew she was dismissed. Her room now her only haven felt cold. Needing something to do, she went through the closet searching for something appropriate to wear to a funeral.

Three days later Mary and her daddy drove to Grandmama's house. Cars filled the yard and driveway. People milled about speaking softly and patting each other's arms.

Dressed like a beauty for the day, Mama stood proud. Her relatives complimented her attire, the loveliness of her mother's home, and the array of food piled in the dining room. As long as she allowed herself the trappings of the perfect hostess, she moved about as if nothing were the matter. Daddy kept a careful eye on her, wondering, Mary supposed, if she would break.

The body was laid out in the parlor in the tradition of the old mountain folk. It sparked conversation in the neighborhood where most people had long ago decided to use the services of the funeral home industry. Grandmama had been adamant that she rest her final moments in the house where she had raised her children, lived her life, and breathed her last. Mama would not betray her mother's wishes no matter whose disfavor it brought down on her head.

Mary noticed Mama's back stiffen and Daddy rush to her side as a woman stepped up to have a go at the bereaved. Mary too, unknowingly, moved in for support as the woman began to speak.

"I am so very sorry about your loss. It's been much too long since we've seen each other!" Putting her gloved hand on Mama's and leaning close, she continued. "We ought not to let a time like this be what brings us back together. How is your father? I hear he ain't too well neither."

As her voice slipped back into the truth of her raising, the woman's meanness became evident. Mary too had wondered about her grandfather but knew she should ask at a better time. The room full of people watched Mama begin to crack and appear to sway toward Daddy's arm. The clearing of his throat was too loud for a time of mourning, cutting like a knife across the biddy's questions. His angry words were stilled by Mama's.

"My daddy is just like he always was. We had to move him into a nursing home. Thank you for asking." She turned to greet the next friend, leaving the onlookers amazed at her panache. Sometimes even Mary was startled by the Southern woman schooled in grace that Mama could become. On most occasions, the social charade angered and frustrated, but every once in a great while it drew the slightness of an evil grin across Mary's lips. For this moment, it caused Daddy to return back to the food, confidence guarding his worry.

Mary's elation was brief. The woman had moved to a group of others. The women's heads drew close as if conspirators making it impossible for Mary to deny her curiosity.

"Did you see that man? And, that child?" "That's her husband and daughter."

"I heard tell she married a darkie, but I couldn't believe it."

Mary couldn't stand to hear more. This was a day of sorrow. She didn't understand the women. People came to offer support, not to cause more harm. She searched for her daddy. He stood back from everyone. His eagle eyes were trained on mama, but he didn't move close to her again. Two more times she joined him and reached for his hand.

The long black hearse came too soon to carry Grandmama's body to the church cemetery. The director spoke for a moment to Mary's father.

Did he think Daddy was part of the crew, Mary wondered. "What is it?" Mama asked.

"We need to stay in another part of the house." Mary's mother's face whitened as she turned to stare at the men coming in with a gurney. "They're taking her now?" she asked. "It's time."

Mary watched her parents embrace while the men bundled Grandmama up and carried her out. Each bang of a door was a slap across Mary's heart. They would no longer be able to drop by for cake and counsel. The garden flowers would wave their dewdrops to another's eye, and Grandmama's kittens would soon run wild again. Fat tears, pooled in sadness, fell like the fearsome sleet that pummeled the windowpanes in the dark cold of winter.

Mary no longer cared how Mama felt; her own pain had become too great. Daddy silently signaled the time had come to leave. Everyone gathered their dress coats, pinned flowers to their chests, and pushed each other into the car for the final journey. Not a word was spoken. Mary watched the people in the world outside the window. They moved about their day, continuing on, not a part of her tragedy. Almost without warning it seemed her thoughts were interrupted and someone was helping her out of the car.

The cemetery had so many wreaths as to look almost festive. The coffin sat atop its hole waiting for the prayers to be said. The family gathered under a circus tent and sat in green felt-covered chairs. It felt odd to Mary to hear people speak of Grandmama as if she were a child or a young woman. Hymns were sung, and some man muttered something about ashes to ashes. Numbly Mary sat until the jarring thump of Grandmama's box hitting the earth caused her to move away. The sun shone hot as the mourners filed away from the scene, smiling and laughing in an attempt to diffuse the pain of the moment. Anger flooded Mary when she heard the backwoods speech of gossip spread more poison through her grandmama's last day.

"Can you believe those coloreds are actually here for the funeral? Look yonder, them there, you see? They talking to them. I told you that man must have African in him.

He's too dark to be all white."

The woman's words caused Mary's eyes to follow the sound, and she saw her father standing with a rather large crowd. Indeed, they were black. Later she discovered the family had come, like the others, to say good-bye to a great woman.

Grandmama had helped her neighbors many times. She cared for sick children, provided food and clothes when needed, and even helped to educate. This had been done neighbor to neighbor, never infringing on anyone's dignity or pride. These people were merely her friends come to offer last wishes and most aware of the need to stand back in their proper place. Grandmama had served them often at her table, unmindful of the unspoken rule of keeping black folks, at the most, on the back porch and preferably out of the main house completely. Their open respect caused Mary to reflect on Mama's ability to marry the savage red man all those years ago. She wondered if it took no strength at all from her mama, only the class of breeding instilled from mother to child and passed down through the generations.

Funny that Grandmama's death gave rise to parts of her that had remained hidden while she walked the earth. Mary was intrigued and felt a measure of pride. She wished she could thank her grandmother for what she had done and the way she had lived.

With the funeral over, the food dishes put away, and the mourners gone, Mary and her parents went home. Mama collapsed on the couch and Daddy covered her with a blanket. Resisting the urge to hold her mama's hand, Mary sat and stared. She prayed Mama would find a way to absorb the hurt.

Sunday would now become the worst day of the week. They all had become used to heading to Grandmama's after church. They could, of course, still go, but why? Mary couldn't stand the lonesome hours of evening as her parents tried to ignore the fact that they were both unable to find any balm to fill the gaping wound in their day. A cold anger swept through Mary's heart as she thought about all that had happened. Her mama stood center with pride. Her daddy stood back, in his place. She merely felt lost.

16

Mary dwelled on events of her life that confused her. She tried to figure out what it meant, what she was supposed to do. Looking for an outlet for all her frustration, Mary found herself searching the library and bookstore shelves for books that held the secrets of her thoughts. She reviewed the world's religions, cults, and promises of the people. Daddy worried more and more about her. Mama tried to steer Mary toward books that would "strengthen" or "teach life lessons."

Walking into the bedroom one afternoon, Mama pulled Mary's book out of her hand. "Just turn the page down and go outside for a little while. You need some air."

"Mama, I'm at a good part," Mary whined.

"Mary, you're reading things that aren't good. What bothers you so?" Mama shrugged, wishing her child would listen.

It was when the books took a turn toward the spirit world that Daddy finally stepped into the fray.

"Mary, why do you want to read such trash as this?"

"Does it scare you, Daddy?"

"Yes, Mary, it does. Did you think I would deny the fear so you could find something to fight about?" He rubbed his hands through his thick black hair, searching, searching for what to say. "Maybe this will give you permission to think less of me? I thought I taught you long ago about the spirit world." Deep in her eyes he searched for understanding. "Those things that keep the human animal on the right track. Have you forgotten?"

"What are you talking about? I only remember the questions left unanswered. The smirk on your face when you told me I would know things when I was supposed to. I'm tired of waiting. This black world interests me. It sparks my imagination, makes me think. How can that be a bad thing?"

"Does it make you believe?" Daddy questioned.

"Believe in what, ghosts and spooks? Reincarnation? Myself and my powers?"

"I don't know, Mary. You tell me. How does it make you feel? Powerful?" He paused. "Or confused?"

"Oh, Daddy, sometimes I feel like a lost little girl. I need answers. I know you love me, but it's not enough anymore."

Daddy shook his head.

"Why won't you and Mama tell me the truth? I've seen so much hate in this town. You won't go to church any more. Mama goes all the time. Look at my skin, Daddy. Look at yours. We're not white.

Tears formed in her daddy's eyes. "Do the children at school tease you? Has someone hurt you?"

"Yes, Daddy." Mary screamed. "You hurt me. Mama hurt me. Why won't you tell me the truth?"

For the first time in her life, she set herself apart from him. She flounced to her room and slammed the door Each night Daddy had tenderly kissed her forehead. It was a ritual of love and comfort. Not this night.

Though she couldn't find the strength to turn to him, when she realized he had slipped out of the room, she wanted to follow him and climb, into his lap, and be his little princess again. She couldn't. A silent scream of torment escaped from her lips and sped headlong into the night.

17

―――◆―――

The next morning,, Mama decided she needed to have a talk with Mary about growing up. It was a little late after all the assemblies the school had sponsored. Still, it provided an interesting start to the day. Mary waited, realizing her mother was nervous and didn't know how to begin. "Mama, I already learned about all the girl stuff and don't have any questions." Her mother appeared relieved but still needing to tell her something.

Finally, with a deep sigh, she asked, "What do you think about having babies?"

Mary blushed. "I guess I never really thought about it much."

Mama brushed back the wayward strands of Mary's hair. "I always wanted a baby, more than anything." She walked toward the door. Mary almost thought she was leaving, but then she propped herself up against the doorway. Gearing up for one of those long speeches that every little girl hates, she waited for attention.

"I thought your daddy wouldn't love me if I couldn't have children. I was too afraid to tell him what the

No Reservations

doctor had told me. It made me so much less of a woman, and it has haunted me my whole life. I guess it's taken me all these years to finally believe that he would stay with me. And of course it took us eight years to finally get you. They wouldn't let us buy any baby stuff. I guess they thought it would be too hard for me to look at for all that time. I guess they knew what was best." Mama paused and looked up at the ceiling for a long time before she continued with a sigh.

"I had to sign a bunch of papers about how I would look after you. They came into our home and inspected us. Sometimes it was a surprise visit. I was always on edge wondering if the house was clean enough, if I looked okay, if Daddy made enough money. They checked our earnings, what we owed, how much insurance we had, everything. I'll never forget the day we picked you up. You were such a tiny thing. Daddy was the one who had to have you. You wouldn't smile at us and seemed sickly to me. I guess that made you a challenge for your father. You know how he loves that. You had on pink clothes and a little pink hat. You know, it really is special to be adopted. For all those people who have babies, they have to take what they get, but we picked you out special. Don't you understand, dear, we picked you out ... special." With that bit of news, she walked out of the bedroom..

Mary sat still as stone. She'd told her friend that Mama wasn't her mama. She knew it to be true but now the notion cut deep. Grandmama was gone and she had no tools to help her absorb the pain. Suddenly, it felt as if she'd lost her mama too. Looking up into the mirror she wished to see inside herself.

"Mary."

As if a puppet on a short string, she turned. "Daddy."

"Your Mama spoke to you?"

"She did." Moments built a wall in the room. "You lied to me.

All these years, you both lied to me."

Daddy's hands balled into fists. "We protected you, looked after you, did what was best."

"Best for me? Best for Mama? Why did you marry her?"

"Because I loved her."

"Our family is a lie."

Daddy stiffened. "Our family is not a lie?"

"Why don't we see your family anymore? If you love Mama so much, why did you stand apart from her at the funeral? Just because you gave up your family and who you are doesn't mean it's best for me to give up too."

"I gave up nothing. I made a good family, a strong family. The world is changing. People are changing. Sometimes choices have to be made, choices that aren't easy."

"Changing? Choices? There's violence on the news every night. Mama can't stand it. Didn't she make you leave you family because of it?"

"Birth pains of a nation, Mary. Out of struggle comes a better world." He forced himself to relax.

No Reservations

"I know Mama was beat before you two were married. I know her papa hated you because you aren't white.

"He simply hated. He didn't need a reason. That's the kind of thinking that allows evil to grow. We've wrapped you in love. You'll have opportunities I never dreamed of."

Mary turned back toward the mirror. Her dark eyes mocked her. She rubbed her face. The harder she rubbed, the redder her skin became.

"Stop that, Mary. You can't rub your skin white."

"I'm not trying to." Abruptly she dropped her hands to her side. "I need to know who I am."

"You are Mary Victoria Smith. You are my bright, beautiful star."

"I know. I'm so special." Her face twisted into a grimace.

"Yes, Mary." Daddy smiled a weak smile. "Don't let hate creep into your heart."

All the tears Mary had shoved away in her life began to flow. Deep sobs shook her shoulders and her hands began to shake. "If I'm so special, why didn't my mother want me?"

"For the same reason we did, Mary. Because she loved you." Mary looked at her daddy's face and saw truth there.

www.ingramcontent.com/pod-product-compliance
Lightning Source LLC
LaVergne TN
LVHW011718060526
838200LV00051B/2939